"Let me hear it again," he said.

I went back to the track and played it again. I started moving my hips in a circular motion, my eyes closed, one hand in the air and an arm around my waist. I got lost in the music. When I opened my eyes, Jackson was watching, studying me. I grabbed his hand and encouraged him to dance with me. He moved a little.

He grabbed my waist with both hands. Much like he had the night of our *almost-kiss*. His body pressed against mine and we danced to the Caribbean beat. With a quick twirl, my back relaxed against him. His arms wrapped tightly around me from behind and I rested my head against his chest. Still moving. Still swaying. My hormones began to rage, and I couldn't think of one place I'd rather be than right there. He planted sweet kisses along the back of my neck, and when I turned to face him, he planted those same kisses on my forehead and nose. Soon, his lips found mine, and this time without interruption. His kiss was gentle, and his tongue found its way between my lips and danced with my tongue. I savored the taste of him.

"You're so damn beautiful," he whispered.

Dear Reader,

It was midbook when I completely fell head over heels in love with Jackson. He's sexy and a generous lover. He's truly a man's man and Jasmine's hero in every sense of the word. She wants a man like her father, and he fits the bill. He needs a woman who can unleash his inhibitions. And Jasmine is exactly that woman.

I hope you will enjoy Jackson and Jasmine's story. Writing this book was effortless and such a joy. Because my family is from the Eleuthera Islands, it was like sitting with them and having a great Bahamian meal while researching the beautiful island they call home.

I hope you absolutely fall in love with the Talbot family! I sure did.

Visit my website at monica-richardson.com or email me at Monica@Monica-Richardson.com.

Happy reading!

Monica Richardson

An
Island
Affair

MONICA
RICHARDSON

HARLEQUIN® KIMANI™ ROMANCE

Recycling programs
for this product may
not exist in your area.

ISBN-13: 978-0-373-86397-6

An Island Affair

Printed in U.S.A.

Monica Richardson writes romance that is based in the Caribbean Islands. Her alter ego, Monica McKayhan, currently has eleven titles in print. *Indigo Summer*, the first book in her young-adult series, was the launch title for Kimani TRU and snagged the #7 position on the *Essence* bestseller list. Monica penned her first romance novel, *Tropical Fantasy*, in 2013.

Books by Monica Richardson

Harlequin Kimani Romance

Tropical Fantasy
An Island Affair

Visit the Author Profile page at
Harlequin.com for more titles

For my Granny, Rosa A. Heggie

(November 1927–2008)

She was special in so many ways, and the
strongest woman I knew. My life is rich because of her.

Acknowledgments

To my husband, the love of my life—
thank you for being my biggest encourager.

To my family and friends—you are my support system.

To my readers who give me the energy to continue
to write, I'm sure you will enjoy the Talbot family
and get to know them well. This is for you!

To my family in the Bahamas—visiting with you and
talking to you about my history has made the research
and writing of this Talbot series a complete joy.

To my agent, Pamela Harty—thanks for years of
support and encouragement. I appreciate you.

Chapter 1

Jasmine

I took the liberty of undressing him. Inch by inch. One piece of clothing after another starting with his tool belt, which I tossed carelessly into the sand. I loosened the belt on his Levi's 501 jeans, slid the zipper down and gently caressed him in places that required careful attention. I lifted his shirt and brushed my hands against his torso. His abs were rock-solid, and his chest protruded against the snug red T-shirt that restrained his biceps. He was gorgeous: a copper-colored man with black curls. I wanted his lips to touch mine, his tongue to dance inside my mouth.

He reached for my hand…and I jolted back to reality.

"I'm Jackson Conner."

I almost missed the introduction. I was too busy fantasizing about him—undressing him in my mind. It seemed unlawful for a man to look like that, to cause things inside of me to react that way.

"Are you Jasmine?" he asked with a bit of agitation in his voice.

"I am...yes." I smiled and took his outstretched hand.

"So you're Edward's little sister," he teased with a smile that was far more beautiful than the ocean that lapped against the shore next to us.

"I'm Edward's sister, yes. Not his *little* sister. As you can clearly see, I'm a grown woman." I lowered my voice almost to a whisper. "Nothing little about me."

I expected Jackson to affirm that I had it going on.

"Just a figure of speech," Jackson muttered.

"Let's just keep it professional, shall we?" I said. "I wouldn't want you getting off course or distracted."

"I'm not easily distracted, and keeping things professional is exactly what I had in mind," said Jackson. "Now if you don't mind, I'd like to go over the construction plans with you."

He delivered his remarks in a businesslike manner. And whatever thoughts I had in my mind about ripping his clothes off quickly disappeared. There were no compliments or acknowledgments. He simply laid out the details of his plans for my family legacy and quickly asked if I had any questions. My immediate opinion was that he was cocky and arrogant. And I didn't particularly care what he thought about me. Not as if I had earlier. In fact, that morning I'd been running behind schedule, not because I was handling other business, but because I'd spent too much time on my appearance. I was glad I'd spent those extra moments. Not because I cared what he thought, but because I now wanted him to see what he couldn't have.

Things had started off smoothly that morning before I left home. As I'd dressed, my hips had swayed to the sounds of Beres Hammond's "I Feel Good." His voice had teased my senses; nostalgia almost brought tears to my eyes. It was great to be home. I missed the Caribbean and everything about it. The music, the food and our family home that rested on the shores of the beautiful ocean. I had grown to love California, but nothing could compare to Eleuthera.

Life in the Bahamas was carefree—magical even. Especially now that the Grove would soon be up and running. The anticipation was like expecting a newborn baby. Not that I would know anything about that. I hadn't yet had the privilege of birthing anybody's child. I didn't even have a man in my life—which was an integral part of having a baby. Though I'd been with my share of guys, I'd only fallen in love with one—Darren, my high school sweetheart.

Darren had always been that guy—the one I'd dreamed of marrying. However, after a surprise visit to Darren's college campus, I quickly discovered that another young woman had become the apple of his eye instead.

As I listened to Jackson, I smoothed down my skirt—the one that hugged my hips so nicely: hips and glutes that I'd worked so hard for the past several months with a personal trainer that I could barely afford. Living in California, I'd felt an enormous amount of pressure to look good and become successful. In less than a year, I'd drained my entire savings trying to achieve both. It was difficult finding work as an actress in a city where everyone was a Hollywood hopeful, and beautiful women were as common as the grains of sand on the beach. Even with confidence and my spicy Bahamian accent, California had proved too challenging and extremely lonely.

I adjusted my long, curly hair, pulling it off the silky, sheer blouse, and caught a whiff of my cologne, again glad I'd taken the time to look my best. First impressions were important. And if I wanted to be taken seriously by our family's contractor and business partner, I had to look the part. No half stepping.

Prior to today's meeting I'd only seen pictures of Jackson Conner. The pictures had been dead-on. The man was definitely a looker. And now as I got a good look at those eyes in person, I was sure they were a color I'd never seen before. Of course I'd seen gorgeous men—LA was full of them—but Jackson was different. He was self-assured and had a commanding presence. He was manly—the type that would grab your hand tightly and lead you to places that you wouldn't normally go on your own. He seemed like the type that made your heart beat at a rapid pace by simply entering the room.

"I was thinking that we'd begin renovation on the first property there," he said as he pointed toward one of the older homes along the beach. "We'll restore the old hardwoods and the cabinetry. It needs a new roof, and we should bring those old windows up to date."

"I think a front porch would be nice. In fact, each home at the Grove should have a front porch."

The Grove was our inheritance—properties that had been passed down from my grandfather Clyde Talbot to my siblings and me. The six of us had collectively decided that the three historical beachfront properties on Harbour Island would be converted into beautiful bed-and-breakfasts. Each would have its own distinct personality, theme and name. The Talbot House would have flair and spunk and boast bright colors. The Clydesdale would have a musical ambience where portraits of jazz and Caribbean music legends would adorn the walls. My grandfather's baby grand piano would reside in the Grand Room of the Clydesdale. And lastly, Samson Place would be the most tranquil of the three homes. Decorated in tropical Caribbean colors, the beachside home would be the most coveted retreat for lovers. The Grove would be a place where tourists could relax and experience the Eleuthera Islands Bahamas in its truest form.

Now as I stood in front of this very gorgeous man—a man I'd be working with for God-only-knew-how-long, spending countless hours with—I knew that this would be a much more challenging task than I'd ever anticipated.

"I agree that each property should have a front porch," said Jackson. "But…"

"And the Clydesdale should have a huge cabana on the back big enough for tables, a fully stocked bar and a dance floor."

"You have a big imagination, it seems," Jackson said.

"Yes, I do. And you should, too, considering you're the engineer of this project." I walked toward the back of the house, and Jackson just stood there. I urged him to come along. "Follow me, and I'll show you exactly where I want the cabana to be."

Jackson followed me, and I wondered if he was enjoying the view of my rear end as we headed to the back of the house. I smiled wickedly at the thought.

"Well," said Jackson, "I can appreciate your ideas for this project, but I have clear guidelines from my commander in chief, Edward."

"I would suggest that you abandon all instructions from Edward and follow my lead from here on out. I'm your new commander in chief. I've been designated to oversee this project."

"Really? See, no one told me that."

"I'm telling you now."

"I'll have a word with Edward about that."

"You should."

"I fully intend to."

"Good."

"Good, then," he finally said.

I'd thrown him off, but I didn't care. He needed to know who was in charge.

"See, right here. I think the space here could be expanded. Perhaps we could build a nice deck. Maybe a nice bar over in that corner, a spacious dance floor right here. I think the dance floor should be the main attraction." I smiled.

"Are you a dancer?" Jackson asked.

"It's one of my favorite pastimes," I said. "And you?"

"I have two left feet."

I wanted to know what his marital status was, but to directly ask him if he was married was rude. He'd think that I was interested in him, and that was the last thing I wanted him to think. So I found the opportunity to ask what I wanted to know.

"Is your wife a good dancer?"

"My wife?"

"Yes. I thought I remembered Edward mentioning that you were married." I lied. Edward and I hadn't discussed much about Jackson, except that he'd be handling the construction of the Grove.

"I'm not," he said, "and have no intentions of ever being married. Women are a bit too high-maintenance for my tastes."

"Really?"

"Yes."

I turned and bumped right into Jackson. Our bodies collided, and he grabbed me to break my fall.

"Sorry," I said as I regained my composure.

"It's those dark shades." He smiled. "How do you even see where you're going?"

"I manage." I was intrigued by his scent, and that gorgeous smile that he kept hidden behind his cool demeanor was a wonderful surprise again.

"Well, good. Now that I know what your ideas are for the cabana, I will try to implement them into the plans. After I speak with Edward, of course."

I rolled my eyes. He wasn't taking me seriously, and I hated it. Jackson's phone rang, and he answered it before I had a chance to respond to his comment. He rudely began a pervasive conversation with the person on the other end of the phone. I'd been dismissed, and I didn't like it one bit. Soon, I'd let Jackson Conner know just how much.

Chapter 2

Jackson

I knew she'd be beautiful, but also superficial and demand that the world revolve around her. I'd met women like her in the past—the ones who spent too much time fishing for compliments. She wouldn't get that from me. I was here to do a job, and I had a personal interest in this project—I'd invested a good portion of my savings. Although I wouldn't be involved in the day-to-day running of the place, the stakes were too high for me to mess around.

The Grove was a promising venture, and when my buddy Edward asked me to invest, I didn't hesitate. He was one of the few people that I trusted. I knew he was a good man and had solid family roots. Edward and I had attended Harvard together and had become instant friends, both very driven and focused, both pursuing a career in politics. Edward had gone on to achieve his political goals. He'd studied law and eventually landed a job in the Florida governor's office.

He worked on President Obama's campaign and now was running for mayor of a small city in Florida. Unlike me, he hadn't given up on his dreams. I envied my old friend, but was proud of his accomplishments. He'd been brave, whereas I'd been a failure. I'd dropped out of law school. Not because my grades were bad (in fact, my grades had been exceptional), or because I couldn't maintain the curriculum. No, I left Harvard because of a lie.

I'd initially chosen Harvard because it was my father's alma mater, a place near and dear to his heart. I remember that the day I got accepted was the proudest day of my life—and his. My father, John Conner, had been my role model, and I wanted to follow in his footsteps. He was a good man, with undeniable character, and taught my brothers and me everything we needed to know about being good men. So it was hard when I discovered that the man who taught me to be honest had been anything but.

It was good that Harvard had been more than just John Conner's alma mater. It was the place where my important friendships were born. It was why I'd come to work at the Grove in the first place and why I had suddenly found myself entertaining Edward's spoiled little sister.

"Let's step inside," I told Jasmine. "It'll be easier for me to show you *my* plans in here."

I grabbed her small elbow to help her climb the stairs of the old house. We stepped inside and the stench of mildew swept across my nostrils as I looked around at the wood paneling on the walls. That would be the first thing to be removed, I thought—wood paneling wouldn't work with my new plans for the place. There were cobwebs in the corners of the ceiling, the baseboards were beginning to rot, and the dull floor needed to be revived. I'd already determined that I could salvage the hardwoods and bring them back to life. In fact, I would preserve as much of the original structure as possible. The Talbot homes were three of the oldest homes on the islands, and the history was undeniable. I thought it an honor to take part in such an important project.

I set my laptop on a dusty old wooden table in the center of the room. I logged in and pulled up the virtual plans that I'd prepared for the renovations at the Grove. With Jasmine standing so close, I tried not to notice the fragrance that was tickling my nose. I ignored the roundness of her behind as she bent over the table, and restrained the mischievous thoughts that suddenly popped into my head. I moved away a bit, put some distance between us.

"I think we'll start here with the Clydesdale." I took her through a virtual tour of the Clydesdale on my computer, which laid out everything from the cracks in the ceiling to the paint on the walls. "The plumbing needs to be redone and the electrical completely rewired. I've got to remove all of the baseboards. They're all rotten. And that paneling on the walls…got to go!"

"What's wrong with the paneling?" she asked. "My great-great-grandfather built this house with his bare hands. I think the paneling adds a nice traditional touch."

"I think this is the twenty-first century and wood paneling played out with eight tracks and platform shoes."

"I think we should try to maintain as much of the integrity of the place as we can. That's what my family wants."

"I didn't get that vibe from Edward when I spoke with him about your family's vision for the place. He and I discussed a more contemporary feel."

She stood straight up, her hand on her hip. It was the first time I really got a good look at her face. *Beautiful* wasn't even the word. She was ravishing. With her mirrored sunglasses, she was a bit too *California* for me, though. But ravishing nonetheless.

"I think I speak for my family and we're looking for a combination of traditional and contemporary. If we make the homes too *twenty-first-century*, then we're no different than the rest of the touristy properties on the island. There's nothing that sets us apart," she said, "but if we maintain some of the property's natural beauty, then we have a niche in the marketplace."

She made a valid point. Maybe she wasn't as clueless as I'd expected. I had gotten the impression from her older brother that she was more of the flighty type.

"I think the Clydesdale should be the most vibrant of the three houses. The colors that you've chosen for your little virtual tour here…they don't really work. I'm thinking bright colors…a very upbeat feel…"

My eyes briefly wandered to the center of her chest, to the perfectly shaped mounds that rested beneath the sheer blouse that she wore. Just a quick glance and I instantly felt guilty about sneaking a peek. It was unprofessional, I knew, but I couldn't help it. She was the type of woman who caused men to stop and take notice of her. I was a structured man—completely focused, but she affected me, caught me off guard. However, I'd never give her the satisfaction of knowing that.

"The cosmetics we can discuss later," I said. "I'm more concerned with the structure and foundation right now."

"We should also talk about renovation time frames. How long will the job take you to complete?" she asked.

"Roughly six months. Maybe more, if I run into anything unforeseen."

"Will you live on the island? Or will you go back to wherever you're from and send orders to your men?"

"I'm from Key West. It's where I was born and raised," I told her. "And as for giving orders to my men…that's not really how it works. And if you must know, I'm a hands-on type of guy. I will oversee the project from start to finish and in most cases, roll my sleeves up and do much of the work myself. My team and I will stay at a local hotel on Harbour Island."

Her cell phone rang, and she glanced at the number on the screen.

"Great, that's good to know." She removed her sunglasses and held her hand out to me. "It was nice meeting you, Johnson. I look forward to working with you."

I took her small hand in mine. "It's Jackson."

"My apologies," she said and then slipped her glasses back on and headed for the door. "Now if you'll excuse me, I think my interior decorator is here."

I watched as she shook hands with the chocolate-colored woman who wore her hair in small braids. As she and Jasmine prattled on about colors and curtains, I pulled my cell phone out, dialed Edward's number.

"Hey, bro, it's Jackson."

"Jackson! What's going on? How are things going at the Grove?"

"Not too bad, but is your sister going to pop up over here every day?"

"Is she causing problems?"

I wanted to say yes! She had me off course with the tight skirt she wore to a construction site. Would she dress like that every day? I wanted to ask him that.

Instead, I said, "She's just got some strong ideas about the renovation. You and I talked about specific things like removing the wood paneling in the Clydesdale, but she thinks the paneling adds character or something. She's already meeting with an interior decorator, and we're nowhere near that point. She's talking about building a cabana on the back of the house, with a bar and a dance floor, and…"

"Jazzy's a little high-strung," said Edward. "I'll have a talk with her."

"Thanks, man. You know I work independently. And you told me I'd have complete control over this project."

"And you will."

He seemed sure of it, and I had no reason to think otherwise. Jasmine needed to be checked early on, so we wouldn't have any problems going forward. The last thing I needed was to have her prancing around in her cute little clothing, barking orders and changing plans that had already been set in stone.

After my chat with Edward, I regained my composure. I hadn't been off balance over a woman in some time. In fact, I'd sworn off women for a while, just until I got my shit together. The women of the world could thank Denise for that. She ruined it for the rest of them. She'd mistaken my kindness for weakness and tried to lock me into an unhealthy relationship for life. She was a liar and had faked a pregnancy just to keep me entwined in her creepy little web of deception. Luckily I came to my senses—but not before she was too far beneath my skin for me to separate the truth from fiction. She'd played me like a fiddle, and I swore that no other woman would get that chance again.

Women couldn't be trusted. Not completely. Even the woman who meant the most to me—my mother—had lied to me. And if you couldn't trust your mother, whom could you trust? I understood her lie, and I'd long forgiven her, but the principle of the matter remained. You want to trust something? Trust your instincts. That's about as far as trust should go. That was my philosophy. It kept you safe, preserved your manhood. Besides, women came with too much baggage. And I had enough of my own baggage. I found that if I kept life simple, worked hard with little time to play, I could truly be happy alone. So I found satisfaction in my work and my company.

Those summers working for a friend of the family had definitely paid off. Jett Prim had owned one of the oldest construction companies in Florida, and he'd taught me everything I knew. I started working for him when I was fifteen years old—the summer before my freshman year in high school. By the end of the summer, I'd saved enough cash to buy an entire new wardrobe. By the next summer, I had enough to purchase my first car—a 1984 Ford Mustang. Candy-apple red with a spoiler on the back. It was a dream car.

My father respected Jett Prim and appreciated him teaching me the importance of hard work. However, he had not been happy with my talk of starting my own construction company.

"Nothing wrong with working with your hands, son. And construction is a good industry, a nice trade to have," he'd say, "but Conner men attend college. It broadens your horizons, multiplies your choices in life. That's what I want for my sons."

Not only did Conner men attend college, they attended the most selective colleges in the country. A Harvard man, John Conner expected nothing less from us. My oldest brother, Eli, graduated from Cornell and was still living in New York with his new wife and child. Sean had chosen the University of Pennsylvania. My parents thought it was because of Penn's engineering program, but the truth was some girl he liked had been accepted there, too. And the two youngest of the bunch—my brother and I—decided to follow in my father's footsteps and attended Harvard. Drew went to Harvard immediately after high school and excelled in their undergraduate program. I completed my undergrad studies at the University of Miami and then was accepted into Harvard Law School.

I loved Cambridge, except for the winters. As a Florida man, I wasn't used to snow and the brisk cold winters in Massachusetts. I preferred to ski across the ocean, not across snowy mountains. Though I loved the thought of snuggling before a roaring fire in the winter, I preferred the warm climate of my hometown. However, I enjoyed my days at Harvard. It was there that I received a quality education and met lifelong friends. Friends like Jack Wesley, who currently had his own law practice, Mike Chancellor, who was a Supreme Court judge, and Stephen Cole, who worked for a prominent finance firm. Edward Talbot, whom I met the first day I set foot on Harvard's campus, was one of my best friends, though. We had been roommates and instant friends—two youngsters with hopes and dreams as big as the earth. We thought we were invincible and we were cocky as hell. Definitely forces to be reckoned with.

Edward was disappointed when I'd announced that I was leaving Harvard. He did everything in his power to convince me to stay—claimed that my reasons for leaving were crazy. That people who were less fortunate would kill for opportunities that guys like us were afforded. He called me ungrateful, selfish and a few other choice words. Which was exactly how I expected him to react. True friends didn't shield you from the truth. They slapped it in your face and that was exactly what he did. Once he discovered that my mind was made up, though, he supported my decision. He hated my decision, but supported it nonetheless. When I became the owner of Prim Construction Company, he sent many clients my way, and now he'd included me in his family's business—the Grove. And for that, I was truly grateful. I would do everything in my power to make it a success.

I didn't have a Harvard law degree, but I had a successful business. After working as Jett Prim's construction manager for a few years, I became the person he trusted to take over the business when he became ill with cancer. He'd never had children, and I was the closest to anyone who resembled a son. He literally placed Prim Construction in my hands. He trusted me, and I swore that I would take care of his baby as if I'd built it myself. So far I'd done just that. I retained his best staff and fired the ones who had made a mockery of this great man for too many years. I did a complete audit of Prim's books and immediately fired his accountant, who had been stealing his profits for more than twenty-five years. In his stead, I hired my Harvard buddy Stephen Cole to get the company's finances in order. Prim Construction began to see growth after that, and I made some smart investments. In the past year, I'd realized profits that had far exceeded what Prim had made during the entire life of the company.

The Grove would prove to be a great investment.

Chapter 3

Jasmine

I'd spent the day rambling through old boxes—boxes filled with family history. My behind was numb from sitting on a wooden crate in the center of the room for the better part of the day. I'd already grown attached to this room. It was the room where my grandfather had been born by the hands of a midwife, and it was the room where his mother had nursed him. With the beautiful sunlight beaming through the window, I imagined my great-grandmother sitting in a chair in the corner of the room and rocking her baby to sleep. The room undeniably had the best view in the house. For that reason, I'd already decided to make it my office during the renovation period, a place where I could work on a marketing strategy for the Grove. A place where I could let my hair down, find myself. Even do some journaling. I'd spotted an old desk in the storage closet that could easily be sanded and finished with little effort. My college roommate had a knack for refinishing old furniture, and she'd taught me a few things. I'd never really refinished anything in my life, but I wanted to. Particularly now, with so many artifacts and pieces of furniture that my grandparents had stored in these houses, I wanted to salvage as much history as I could.

I dug into another box, sorting through all of the old black-and-white photographs of my ancestors—generations of people who existed long before my grandfather. His father's father and beyond.

I smiled at photos of my father and his siblings. I gently eased my finger across the photo I found of my parents. They couldn't have been more than twenty-one, both young students at Howard University, where they met and fell in love while Mother studied to become a teacher and Daddy studied medicine. After graduating medical school, Daddy landed a residency at a hospital in Key West, over a thousand miles from his new girlfriend, who was offered a teaching position at a prestigious school in Maryland, near her hometown of DC. It appeared that this was the end of their love affair, as neither of them wanted to hinder the other's career.

Confident that he'd made the most practical decision, Daddy took a train back to Key West, leaving my mother behind. He'd managed to bury himself in his work, yet his heart still longed for her. When she showed up in the emergency room of his hospital, with bags in tow and a swollen belly, he was happier than any man could be. She was carrying my oldest brother, Edward. Daddy's life changed completely that night.

My parents had such a wonderful love story—the kind you found in romance novels. I hoped to find such a love one day. A man like my father, Paul John Talbot, who would sweep me off my feet. It was no doubt my father had been a great catch. Why else would my mother show up at his hospital like that in the middle of the night? He was a great husband and I knew firsthand that he was a great father.

"Excuse me," a voice interrupted my daydreaming. Jackson Conner.

"Yes?" I said.

"It's getting late. It's just about sunset, and my guys are packing up. We're about to head out for the day," said Jackson. "Can I see you to the water taxi?"

"Uh, no." I stood up and smoothed my skirt and adjusted my blouse. I'd become too relaxed. Had I known I'd be going through old boxes, I would've worn a pair of old jeans. "I'll be wrapping up here soon."

"Okay, I'll wait, then…while you gather your things."

"It's not necessary," I said. "You go on. I'll be fine."

"I would really like to secure the place before I leave and make sure you're home safely. This is really not a place to be hanging out. There's hazardous stuff everywhere."

"This is my home. This island, I mean. I know it like the back of my hand. I know just about every person—every family here. And I'm not a child. I know better than to mess with hazardous materials." I placed the photographs back into the box. "But thanks for your concern."

"Fine," Jackson said, "stay here, then."

"I'll be fine. And I'll secure the place," I said.

Jackson turned to walk away without another word.

"Oh, by the way," I called to him, "there's an old desk in the storage shed. Can you have one of your guys bring it up here for me? This room will be my office during the renovation."

"Why?" he asked.

"Why what? I need a place to work."

"I don't think that's a good idea. You being here during the renovation will just interfere with our work."

"I won't interfere with your work. You won't even know that I'm here," I told him. "You can just work around me. But I want to be here."

"I'm not comfortable with that." From the look on his face, Jackson was becoming unnerved. But I didn't care. Who was he to tell me where I could or could not be?

"Sorry about your discomfort, but I'll be here every day from now on. So you probably should get used to seeing my face around here." I gave him a wicked smile.

"Good night, Miss Talbot." His face was hardened and his jaws were clenched before walking away.

I was under his skin. I could tell.

"I'll lock up when I'm done here," I yelled to him.

He kept walking, never responded. I heard his footsteps on the stairs and then the front door shutting. Not only had I gotten to him, I had to admit Jackson Conner got on my nerves, too. Who did he think he was anyway? And he may have made an investment in the property, but for him to tell me how often I could be on the premises of my family's inheritance was ludicrous. I'd address that with Edward the next time we spoke.

I went back to sorting through old photos and remembered when we first heard about the Grove. Our parents had commissioned the six of us back to the islands—our home—for a family meeting. The news of the inheritance took us all by surprise, and everyone expressed strong opinions about what should be done with the properties. My brother Nate immediately suggested that we sell the properties and split the proceeds. He had no intentions of returning to the Bahamas long-term. Atlanta, Georgia, had long become his home and a place where he'd built a wonderful career as an artist. The Bahamas held too many bad memories for him, and even coming home for this family meeting had been a struggle.

I, on the other hand, had great memories of home and immediately thought that the family should convert the old houses into bed-and-breakfasts. I knew that the Bahamas was a beautiful, tourist-driven place, and such a business would generate a nice income for all six of us—an income that I desperately needed in my life at the moment.

"Who has time to run a bed-and-breakfast, let alone three of them?" asked Alyson, my oldest sister, who was the successful real-estate agent in the family. "I certainly don't. I'm with Nate. I say we revitalize the properties and place them on the market. I can have a solid contract on them in no time."

"I definitely can't move to the islands right now. I'm up for reelection!" exclaimed Edward. "But I have a friend who owns his own construction business. He can definitely do the work. I'll fly over and assist as much as I can, but I can't move here."

Finally we agreed that we weren't going to sell the properties, but develop them. We wanted to honor our father's wishes—to do something great with the properties, as he'd suggested. But the reality was, the properties would require more time and effort—not to mention resources—than any of us would be able to provide alone.

"I like Jasmine's idea of developing the properties into bed-and-breakfasts. And I think we should call it the Grove," said my sister Whitney. "I'd be happy to help run the place when the school year ends." Whitney had gone to college in Dallas, Texas, and never returned to the Bahamas. Instead, she'd accepted a teaching position at an elementary school there and made her home in a cozy little Dallas suburb.

My youngest brother, Dennison, had been as quiet as a church mouse for most of the conversation. As the baby of the family, he was often forgotten.

"Denny, you haven't said what you think about all of this," I said. "What would you like to see happen with the properties?"

"I don't really care one way or the other," he said.

"I think if we do this bed-and-breakfast thing, Denny could probably play a major role in running the place," suggested Alyson, "especially since he's the only one who lives at home right now."

"No," said Denny.

"Why not?" asked Alyson. "You're not doing anything else! It's not like you're going to college."

Dennison, who had been a few weeks from graduating high school, hadn't yet identified a school of higher education.

"Of course he's going to college," said Nate, the ever-protective brother. "He just hasn't figured out where. Get off his back!"

"I haven't applied anywhere because I'm not going to college," said Denny matter-of-factly.

The entire household fell silent. No one said anything for what seemed like a lifetime. We all waited for hell to break loose.

My mother, who hadn't said much either, stood with her hands on her hips. "Dennison Talbot, what do you mean you're not going to college?"

We waited for Denny's response.

"I've enlisted in the Royal Bahamas Defence Force. I've already sworn in, and after graduation, I'm due to be deployed to the United States to train with the US Navy Seals."

"Have you lost all the sense God gave you, child?" My mother's Bahamian accent suddenly seemed stronger than normal. It usually came and went, considering she wasn't a native. She turned to my father. "Paul John, did you hear what your son just said?"

"Daddy." Denny tried to whisper, but failed. "You said you would talk to her."

"You knew about this, Paul?" she calmly asked my father.

"Beverly, this is not the time for this discussion," my father said calmly. "Not while we're discussing the children's inheritance. One issue at a time."

"This discussion is not over." She pointed a finger at Denny and then at my father. "We will revisit it."

With Denny going away soon, the idea of turning the properties into a successful business had seemed impossible, particularly since we were all scattered about the US. Pulling this off would require a sacrifice that no one was willing to make—except for me. Having had very little success as a model-turned-actress, I was ready to return home.

"I'll do it," I volunteered. "I'll move back home and oversee the construction. And I'll even write the business and marketing plan."

"Have you ever written a business plan before, Jasmine?" asked Alyson.

"Yes, at Spelman," I told her. My classes in college had equipped me with a great deal of business knowledge.

"Have you ever written a real business plan for a real business, I mean?"

"Well, no…"

"Where have you used what you learned at Spelman? In Hollywood?" Alyson continued.

I rolled my eyes at my sister, who'd obviously found humor in the fact that I'd chosen a different career path than the rest of my siblings.

A few hours later, I placed the photos back into the boxes I'd found them in. It was getting late, and I needed to make my way to the water taxi before nightfall. I did a final walk-through of the house, shut off all the lights, secured the place and then stepped outside.

I was surprised to find Jackson seated on a stoop outside, chattering on his phone.

"What are you still doing here?" I asked him once he'd wrapped up his call.

"I had a few loose ends to tie up."

"You sure you aren't stalking me?"

"Of course not. I have better things to do than to stalk you."

"I told you I'd be fine," I said.

"I know, but I wanted to make sure anyway."

"Fine. I'm leaving."

"Good."

I smiled as I hopped into the backseat of the cab. Of all those bad qualities I'd pinpointed in Jackson, I could not accuse him of not being a gentleman.

Chapter 4

Jasmine

My father stood at the dock with his graying sideburns, tall, slender frame and round midsection. He wiped sweat from his dark brown face with a handkerchief and grinned a wide grin when he saw me.

"Hello, darling," his deep voice greeted me.

"Hi, Daddy." I hugged my father. "You didn't have to pick me up. I could've gotten a taxi."

I was happy to see my father. It reminded me of the times he'd picked me up from school when I was much younger. He'd stand outside the little pink schoolhouse and wait to walk me home. I'd tell him all about my day, and we'd stop for fresh fruit at the market—papayas, mangoes and pineapples.

"It's okay. Your mother sent me to the market anyway. I think she wanted me out of the house—sometimes I get on her nerves, if you can believe that."

"I don't believe that." I laughed.

"It's true." Daddy laughed heartily. "Besides, I couldn't wait to find out how things went at the Grove today. I'm so proud of you, and your brothers and sisters for taking this on." He had a strong Bahamian accent, though he was not born or raised in the Bahamas. He grew up in Key West. But with both parents of Bahamian descent, he was bound to speak just like them.

My siblings and I had Bahamian accents as well, although I tried with all my might to lose mine once I left the islands. And with California being a huge melting pot, my accent was just one of many dialects there.

"I found all sorts of things belonging to Grammy and Granddad. Photos and paintings and stuff. Lots of photos of Granddad and his band."

My father smiled.

"My father was a multitalented musician. He played the trumpet, traveled throughout the Caribbean with his band. He played the goombay drums, and when he lived in Key West, he was a self-taught pianist. He had his very own baby grand piano and had it shipped over from the States."

"I saw the baby grand. It's beautiful! I think it will look nice in the Clydesdale," I said. "I guess I got my desire for the arts from him."

"I guess you did." Daddy held my car door open and I hopped in.

He maneuvered the car on the left side of the road and navigated down Queen's Highway from the water-taxi dock toward our home on Governor's Harbour.

"I'm really not feeling Edward's friend Jackson, the contractor…" I lowered my window a bit to catch a breeze, checked my hair in the side mirror. "He's so…let me see…" I thought about the words I wanted to use. "…so arrogant and egotistical."

"Really?"

"Yeah, I don't like him much at all. I don't know if I can work with him," I said. "Maybe we can find someone who's a little more approachable to do the work. Someone friendlier."

"Is he unapproachable?"

"He's cold. Self-absorbed."

Daddy smiled a little. "You mean he didn't make a fuss over you."

"What? No. I don't care about that," I said. "I just care about the Grove and making sure we've hired the best person for the job."

"He has a very impressive work history and comes highly recommended."

"Of course he's highly recommended by Edward—they're friends!"

"By people he's done work for in the past." Daddy pulled his old pickup truck in front of the house, a vehicle he'd owned for as long as I could remember. "From what I can tell, the fellow does excellent work. You should do a little research on him. You'd be surprised at what you'll find."

I climbed out of the truck and gave the door a hard push. "Maybe I will."

I found Denny in his bedroom, lying flat on his back and tossing a football into the air.

"Don't you have anything better to do?" I peeked inside.

"No." He was so unconcerned. He'd recently made one of the biggest decisions of his life and seemed so dispassionate about everything else.

"You seem so weird lately, like it doesn't concern you that you'll be deployed soon."

"It's life, Jazzy. No big deal."

"No big deal? Really?" I took a seat at the foot of his

bed. "Well, if it's no big deal, why didn't you tell our parents about it before you did it?"

"Because they make a big fuss about everything! I mean, I'm just not college material. I know my limitations. I know what I want, and this is it. End of story."

"Aren't you a little bit afraid?"

"Of course. I mean, weren't you afraid when you went away to Spelman? And weren't you afraid when you moved to California?"

"Terrified."

"Well, I'm not terrified. But I'm a little scared," he admitted. "But it's my life. And no one can live it for me."

"You're right." I smiled. "I guess you're not a little kid anymore. You're growing up. You obviously trusted Daddy enough to talk to him about this. I think Daddy's easy to talk to."

My brother gave me a sideways glance. "He's easy for you to talk to. You're his favorite."

"What?"

"Yeah…you didn't know?"

"I'm not his favorite. He loves all of his children equally."

"Well now, that might be true. But he's not as easy as you think he is. Not with me. When all of you guys left for college, it was bad. I received everything that was meant for all of you. The good and the bad. Mostly the bad," Denny laughed. "Every time one of you messed up, or made a bad decision, I caught hell. All of the lessons you missed, I got them. So unfair."

"You're exaggerating." I grabbed a pillow and threw it at my little brother.

"Oh yeah, I caught hell for you more than anybody!" Denny laughed a bit. "Jasmine this, Jasmine that. Jasmine broke up with Darren, and now her grades are bad. Jasmine moved clear across the country to California. Who does she know there? Where will she stay? How will she pay her rent? Denny, no, you can't go out with your friends. We have to figure out what we're going to do about Jasmine."

"Shut up!" I laughed.

"I'm serious. You're responsible for my lack of a decent social life. They sheltered me from your mistakes."

"You're exaggerating."

"You always were the rebel," said Denny, "which is why the rest of them don't think you can handle the Grove. It's why they give you such a hard time. They're jealous of you. Wish they could be rebels, too."

I was laughing hard at this point. "You think so?"

"I know so!" said Denny. "It's true because I wanted to be like you, too. I admire you, Jazzy. You follow your dreams. Even if things don't work out for you, at least you give it a try."

"Oh, Dennison Talbot. You are a sweetheart." I grabbed my little brother's face in my hands and kissed his forehead.

"I'm serious. It's why I joined the Royal Bahamas. I'm making a bold move to do what I want to do."

"I'm happy that you're doing what makes you happy, Denny." I smiled. "When do you ship out?"

"Few weeks." He walked over to his computer desk, pulled out a blue velvet box and handed it to me.

I opened the box and was astonished to find a beautiful diamond ring inside.

"Why, Dennison Talbot! I don't know what to say." I covered my chest with my hand.

"Shut up!" He snatched the ring. "It's for Sage."

"Of course it is. You've only dated her since the sixth grade."

"I want you to hold on to it for me. And if I come back—"

I raised an eyebrow at his choice of words. "*If* you come back?" I asked.

"I mean, when I come back I'm going to ask her to marry me. You're the only one that I trust with this." He handed the ring back to me.

"I feel so honored."

"No, seriously, I don't want anyone else to know."

"I won't tell a soul. I promise." I gave my little brother the biggest hug. He was growing up right before my eyes. I stuffed the velvet box into the pocket of my skirt and gave Denny a warm smile as I walked toward the door. "I love you, big head."

"I love you back."

I left his room and headed down the hall to my own private space. My room hadn't changed much. With two comfortable canopy beds, two chests of drawers and an old white pine desk in the corner of the room, it was the place I'd shared with my younger sister, Whitney. Things were just as we'd left them when I went away to Spelman, and she went away to college in Texas. Old-school posters of Caribbean artist Elephant Man still adorned my side of the wall, reminding me of my high school party days. My brother Nate and I would sneak off to the neighboring islands without my parents' knowledge. We'd make up the excuse that we were spending the night with friends. We were clever and kept our sister Whitney as our watchperson.

Whitney had never been one to attend parties—or to sneak away, for that matter. She was the practical, levelheaded one of the Talbot bunch, always the peacemaker, always finding the good in everyone. Perfect attributes for a kindergarten teacher. Through Whitney, my mother was able to live her teaching dreams vicariously. And for that reason, she had clearly become my mother's favorite. I was probably my mother's least favorite of the bunch, having disappointed her on more than enough occasions. She was a worrier, and I'd caused her the most angst. She was convinced that I'd thrown away my education when I went traipsing across the country to pursue an acting career.

"Do you know how many people have rushed to Hollywood, looking to become famous?" she'd asked me. "You have a good education, from a good school, and yet you choose to squander it."

I never changed my course. I still moved to California. However, my mother's words stuck with me. She probably thought I didn't listen to her, but the truth was I listened to everything my parents taught me. Kept all their instruction tucked away for safekeeping and pulled things out as I needed it.

I stuck Denny's velvet box beneath my mattress, sat on my bed and glanced over at Whitney's side of the room. Her stupid teddy bear Georgie relaxed atop her pillow—his place for most of her life. She couldn't sleep without him. I missed Whitney. I missed Alyson, too. As young girls, we were all much closer—having shared so many intimate secrets growing up. Alyson was my first best friend, my accomplice on many of my sneaky endeavors. I'd been close with both my sisters.

I removed the embellished sandals from my feet and changed into a pair of exercise pants and a tank top. I turned on my music playlist on my iPhone, rolled my mat onto the hardwood floor and immediately began to stretch my limbs. As I worked out the kinks in my body, thoughts of Jackson Conner entered my head, unannounced. Unwarranted thoughts danced about without permission. Despite his arrogance, the man was so sexy. I smiled at the thought of him wanting to see me to the ferry. That was cute. Actually it was quite gentlemanlike, I thought. It was surprising that a man like him would care at all. He seemed so pompous.

I got into the downward-dog position, stretched my body across my mat. Yoga was a practice that I'd studied and developed as a significant part of my lifestyle. My parents didn't understand yoga.

"We're Baptists," my mother reminded me when I tried to explain what all the stretching and candle-lighting was about, "and we don't practice any other religions in this house!"

It was a lost cause trying to explain to them that yoga was not a religion. So I simply exercised behind closed doors, and very quietly. But I made a mental note that, as much as I loved my childhood home, I needed my own place very soon.

Chapter 5

Jackson

I could see the flames in the distance and hear the sirens blare. I felt helpless in the backseat of the taxi, so close to the Grove. Though I wanted the driver to speed up a bit, that would never happen. No one on this island hurried for anything. Relaxed and easygoing, the islanders fished, took long walks along the beach and lounged on hammocks all day. *Hurry* was not a part of the culture here. My heart pounded and my mind raced as I thought of the Grove. The electrician was scheduled to be at the properties this morning. Had there been a mishap? A short circuit? I prayed.

When I pulled up at the Clydesdale, my men were already on the scene and work had already begun. And I was relieved to know that the fire was about a mile farther down the road at one of the local vacation homes. I exhaled as I stepped out of the backseat of the cab and paid the driver. A quick glance and I spotted her, not that I was looking for her. Although she wore a pair of tight jeans and a faded T-shirt, she was still just as beautiful as the day before. My energy changed. She made me sweat and caused my heart to beat a little faster. I was nervous for no reason at all, and I didn't like it. No man should feel that way around a woman, unless she's Beyoncé or Halle Berry. Jasmine Talbot wasn't a celebrity. She was a wannabe.

She stood in front of the house chatting with my construction manager, Lance. Pointing her finger up at one of the windows, it seemed she was giving him orders and that was completely out of the question. Whatever she wanted done, she needed to address it with me. And I would tell her so, just as soon as I was able to peel my eyes from her and gather my thoughts. I found myself wondering how old she was, as if it mattered. I knew she was Edward's younger sister and he was my age. I'd recently celebrated my twenty-ninth birthday—two months before his. So she couldn't have been much younger than that.

"Is there something I can assist you with, Miss Talbot?" I interrupted her little meeting.

"I was just explaining to Lance here that I'll be working in that room up there—" she pointed upward again "—and he's agreed that he'll have someone bring the old desk out of the storage shed for me…and place it in my office."

"Miss Talbot—"

"Jasmine," she interrupted. "Call me Jasmine please."

"Jasmine." I faked a smile. Chose my words carefully. "You asked me about that desk yesterday…"

"Yes, and I didn't like your response."

"If you don't mind, please do not address my men. If you have an issue or concern, I would appreciate if you would take it up with me."

"I would've done that, Mr. Conner—"

"Jackson," I corrected her.

"I would've done that, Jackson. But you weren't here."

"I'm sorry I was a bit late. I was detained. Stomach-ache. Had to settle my…" Why was I explaining this to her? "I'll make sure the desk is carried upstairs for you."

"Thank you, Jackson." She walked away, headed inside and then turned back to me, catching me staring at her. "Lemon and warm water," she said.

"Excuse me?"

"Best thing for an upset stomach. My mother used to give it to us all the time. Settles it right away."

"Thank you," I said, but she was already gone. I glanced over at Lance, who was also staring at Jasmine. "Close your mouth."

"I think she likes me." Lance smiled.

I laughed and handed him a set of plans I'd revised. "Here. I've revised these. The wood paneling on the wall in the great room stays. And when you get a chance, have a couple of the guys bring that cruddy old desk out of the storage space and take it up to that room. Let's get the room painted and the floors done right away. Maybe that'll keep her out of our hair."

"I don't mind her being in my hair," said Lance with a huge smile.

I gave him a sideways look and he wiped the grin from his face.

"I'm on it," he said.

"Thanks."

"Oh, and Jax," said Lance, "let's not drink so much tonight."

"I'm not drinking with you fools at all…ever again," I said, "and contrary to popular belief, we're not on this glorious, wonderful, magnificent island for a vacation. We're here to work! That's it."

"What? All work and no play? That's boring. No wonder you can't find a woman. You're a workaholic."

"I'm not looking for a woman. I'm happy, see?" I faked a smile.

"Right." He shook his head and walked away.

He was right. I was a workaholic—a lifestyle that I'd developed at a very young age. Ambition didn't allow for much sleep or playtime. Even in my sleep I dreamed of success. And playtime consisted of an occasional eighteen holes on the golf course with a few of my college buddies. Being a workaholic had everything to do with why I didn't have a woman in my life. Women required things that I wasn't prepared or willing to give them— time. And I didn't have much of it. When I was at home in Key West, after a hard day's work, I usually settled into my renovated bungalow in Old Town. With a cold bottle of Heineken and takeout from a local eatery, I normally watched SportsCenter or caught a game on ESPN, with my laptop in front of me as I simultaneously reviewed plans and designs. I lounged in my leather easy chair in the corner of the room, where I almost always fell asleep before finally going to bed. It was my routine.

Since being on Eleuthera, I'd been having a hard time finding my rhythm. My vacation rental home was a far cry from my bungalow in the city. Although it was a gorgeous place, with its similar pastel-colored homes as the ones in Key West, Eleuthera was not my home.

Last night, I'd allowed my staff to twist my arm and I'd reluctantly stepped outside of my comfort zone. I ventured to a local bar on Harbour Island and found every one of my employees there. They were loud and boisterous and encouraged me to be the same. My good senses told me to rule against it, but I didn't listen. I started the night with a cold beer at the opposite end of the bar as them, wanting to alienate myself from the rowdiness. I rarely drank more than a beer or two, but my first few days on the island had proved to be somewhat trying. I'd had to work out a few details with the town planning board and Ministry of Works, make sure the proper permits were in place, bring my new hires up to speed. And then there had been a small fire, caused by improper electrical wiring, and one of my best workers had injured his hand. A trying week at best, and bumping heads with Jasmine Talbot hadn't helped one bit.

By the end of the night, I had given in to the peer pressure. Taken too many tequila shots, trying to keep up with guys much younger than me. And now I was definitely paying for that decision. The morning sunshine creeping in my window had greeted me with a harsh headache and stomach pains. My ulcer screamed at me. I cursed Lance and the other guys all the way to the bathroom. But as I'd stared at the reflection looking back at me in the mirror, I knew exactly who was to blame.

As I stood in front of the Clydesdale, my phone rang. I looked at my mother's face on the screen as a Jay-Z tune played—my ringtone. Jay-Z had been one of my favorite contemporary artists since Harvard. His music had gotten me through some of my most challenging days. However, I preferred old-school artists—Sugar Hill, Run DMC, Big Daddy Kane—that my older brothers listened to, and, unlike them, I liked jazz. But because they considered it an old man's music, I didn't let on.

I declined the call from my mother. I wasn't ready to talk yet. When my phone rang again, I answered. One of my suppliers I'd been waiting to speak with for two days was finally getting back to me. As I talked and paced back and forth, Jasmine walked past—headed up the road. Those jeans hugged her in all the right places, and her shirt crept up her back with each step. I forced myself to look away. Why was I even checking her out? I would never date anyone so self-centered. She wasn't my type at all. Of course, she was attractive, and I only dated attractive women. But she was all over the place, wasting an education and running off to Hollywood to chase a pipe dream of being an actress or a model. And as soon as things didn't work out, it seemed that she'd rushed back home to the islands to live off her parents again. Why would I be checking out a woman with no stability and misguided ambitions? That wasn't the type of woman I would have in my life. Not that I was looking for one. A woman like that was sure to be unhappy with my work schedule. Depending on the job, I was often gone for months at a time, and I kept late hours, never leaving a job site until the work was done. My business came first, no matter what, so there was no room in my life for a high-maintenance female.

I made a few more calls, and then I caught myself watching Jasmine again as she moseyed back down the road.

"Here you go," she said, handing me a disposable cup with a lid.

"What's this?"

"Warm water and lemon," she said. "I ran to the little restaurant just down the way."

"Really? Thanks."

"You're welcome. Hope you feel better."

Answering her ringing phone, she started chattering with someone on the other end and took off for the house. I was moderately touched by her act of kindness.

I watched as she walked into the house, couldn't take my eyes off of her. But then I chastised myself for looking at what I couldn't have. And didn't want.

Chapter 6

Jasmine

The old wood on the kitchen floor had been revived. The walls had been sanded but not painted yet. The only appliance was an antique gas stove, which needed to be cleaned. I rolled up my sleeves, put on a pair of rubber gloves and commenced to clean it. I had my work cut out for me, and it took the better part of the morning to get the stove to usable condition.

As a gesture of goodwill, I'd decided to prepare lunch for Jackson's team. It was impulsive, I knew it, but I wanted to show them how much I appreciated them for tending to all my little requests. Jackson hadn't been the friendliest person, but his guys had been more than helpful and accommodating since they'd started work on the Grove. They'd moved things around and carried heavy furniture to places where I needed it. I'd chatted with a few of them during their smoke breaks, given advice about women, laughed at their jokes. We'd become great friends in a short time, to Jackson's dismay. Occasionally he'd walk past while I joined them during their breaks and scowl at us. Every one of them expressed that Jackson was a workhorse and needed to loosen up, but despite that, they had the utmost respect for the man who paid them very well and loved them like family.

"He has a hard exterior, but a big heart," said Jorge one afternoon while taking a puff on his Marlboro. "Last Christmas when I was having a hard time financially, Mr. Conner bought Christmas gifts for all four of my children. Dirt bikes, Tonka trucks, dolls, a PlayStation…even clothing. He left it all on our back porch on Christmas Eve. Sent me a text message and told me to go look outside. It meant the world to me and my wife. It was a great gesture."

"When my mother was about to lose her home, Mr. Conner made a few calls to some of his buddies at City Hall and turned everything around for her," said Diego. "She makes him pulpeta at least once a month."

"Pulpeta?" I asked.

"Cuban meat loaf," Diego said matter-of-factly. "Meat loaf is his favorite."

I was startled to hear all of the admirable things that Jackson had done for his employees, particularly since I hadn't seen that side of him. The side of Jackson that I'd experienced had been far from admirable.

I finished cleaning the old stove. Then I fired it up to make the men an authentic Caribbean lunch. I prepared conch salad, conch fritters, Bahamian spiced chicken and cassava bread. On the old folding table Jorge had pulled out of the closet for me I placed the platters on a crisp white tablecloth along with two candles and fresh flowers in a vase that I'd found.

I plugged my docking station into the wall and searched

for a nice Caribbean playlist. Something upbeat and contemporary. I found a nice mix of Caribbean rhythms and pumped up the volume.

"It's time!" I yelled.

"Time for what?" Lance removed his hard hat and gave me a wide grin. A tall, light brown, thin man, Lance was a flirt, and I was careful not to give him false hope.

"I prepared lunch for everyone," I told him.

"Really?"

"Yes, and it's getting cold. So, let's go!"

"Jackson ran out for a bit," Lance explained. "Had to meet with a supplier."

"It's okay. We'll put a plate aside for him."

"I don't know if he'll appreciate us eating and listening to music and stuff on the job…"

"You're not allowed to eat and listen to music on your lunch break? You do get a lunch break, don't you?" I asked. "US labor laws require that you get at least thirty minutes. I'm sure Bahamian laws are much looser."

"We do get a lunch break. It's just that it's still early. We don't usually break until around one."

"So make an exception today. What's the big deal?"

Lance looked around as if he was contemplating my question. Then loudly he made the announcement to his crew. The men slowly began to gather in the dining room.

"Miss Talbot made lunch for us…" he began.

"Jasmine," I corrected him. "I'm just Jasmine."

"Jasmine made lunch for us. And we're going to break a little early," said Lance. "But thirty minutes is it, guys. Then it's back to work."

As soon as he made the announcement, the men went for the food like gluttonous beasts, piling up their plates as if they hadn't eaten in days. As they ate, I began to move my hips to the music, even sang some of the words.

Although I'd never been much of a singer, I didn't let that stop me. I knew how to have fun. Jorge started dancing with me, balancing a plate of food in his hand, and before long, everyone was moving at least one or more parts of his body.

"I like how you move, girl!" said Tristan, the blond young man who'd only recently graduated high school. Laughter filled the room at his remark. "I wish I was a little older."

"And what would you do if you were older, Tristan?" I teased.

"I'd make you my wife." He grinned. "You're beautiful!"

"And you are a sweetheart," I said. "Come dance with me."

"Tristan can't dance," said Diego. "He has two left feet."

"Of course he can dance," I insisted. "There's no right or wrong, as long as you're having fun."

I motioned for Tristan to join me on our makeshift dance floor—a small area just between the kitchen and dining area. He found his way to me and started moving, but he was so focused on his feet that he looked as if he was in pain.

"Don't look at your feet, honey. Just let your body move with the music. Just be free with it."

"Like this?" he asked, his hips still stiff.

"Keep trying. You'll get it." I closed my eyes and continued to sway.

Suddenly the music stopped and I opened my eyes to see Jackson standing across the room, a frown on his face.

"What the hell is this?" he asked.

"Why did you unplug my music?" I ignored his ques-
~ and asked my own. I was livid.

~nce, what is this?" Jackson ignored me. Instead he

turned to Lance, who looked like a cat who'd swallowed a canary.

"It's called lunch." I said it so Lance didn't have to.

"I was speaking to my construction manager, if you don't mind."

"Frankly I do mind," I said. "The men are entitled to a lunch break, aren't they?"

"Yes, but on my terms. Not yours."

"So you decide when grown men eat lunch?" I asked.

"I'm done having this conversation with you," said Jackson and then he turned to his men. "Finish up and get back to work!"

He gave me a look of dismay and then pulled Lance aside. He was cool and calm, but he appeared to be giving his construction manager a reprimand. I felt sorry for Lance. The men slowly started to move back to their working positions.

"Thanks for lunch, Miss Talbot," said Diego. "Everything was delicious."

Tristan kissed my cheek. "You're a great cook and a great dancer."

"You're going to make some man very happy someday, *mi querida*." Jorge gave me a wink and a warm smile.

"Thank you, baby." I pressed my hand against Jorge's rugged face.

"May I speak with you, Jasmine?" asked Jackson.

He didn't wait for my response, just stormed past me. I followed the very angry man into the kitchen, and once we were both there, he turned to face me.

"I think we would get along much better if you would allow me to handle my staff. I'm very close to asking you to leave this property."

"Excuse me?" I frowned. "You don't have the authority to ask me to leave this property. In case you've forgotten, this is *my* family's property. Therefore, you work for my family. Thus, you work for me. Not the other way around."

"For your information, I do have authority here. I have a stake in this property. I've invested a considerable amount of my own assets into this project."

"Let's get one thing straight, Jackson Conner. You might control those men out there, but you sure don't control me. I can do whatever I please, and there's nothing you can say or do about it."

"I'm not trying to control you, but I am trying to run a business and I can't have my men all over the place. We're here to work, not dance to Caribbean music and party in the middle of the afternoon. This isn't Hollywood. This is real life. And you should take it more seriously."

"Maybe you should take it less seriously," I said. "How dare you judge me?"

"I'm not judging you. Only speaking the truth," he said. "Maybe if you'd taken your education more seriously, you'd be working at some high-level company right now and not here cramping my style."

"You don't know anything about me, you pompous… arrogant…"

He walked out of the kitchen before I could finish my sentence, and I followed.

"Don't you dare walk away while I'm still talking!"

"This conversation is over, Miss Talbot."

"Oh, you can dish it out, but you can't take it when someone else gives it to you," I said.

"Stay away from my men, or I'll have you removed from this property."

"You just try it."

He continued to walk out the front door, although I had so much more to say. My blood began to boil, and my heart pounded. My hands were balled into tight fists. I hated him. Wanted to punch him in the face. Wanted to kick him in places where it hurt. Wanted to tackle him to the floor. Wanted to wipe that gorgeous smile and those beautiful eyes from my mind. Wanted to kiss those horribly sexy lips—and I hated myself for even thinking it.

I spent the remainder of the afternoon cleaning the kitchen and putting food away. Busywork always helped me to calm down. I just wanted to stay out of Jackson's way and avoid another confrontation with him.

His presence was totally unexpected when he showed up in the kitchen.

"Jasmine." His voice startled me. "I'm heading out for the day. I just wanted to say good-night and to tell you… um… I wanted to apologize for earlier. I was out of line and said some things that I probably shouldn't have said. I'm sorry."

I was shocked by his apology. Speechless. Before he came in, I was ready to give him the *you-don't-know-what-you're-talking-about* speech and the *who-do-you-think-you-are-anyway* speech. There were so many things I'd planned to say the next chance I got—most of which were no longer appropriate, because Jackson Conner had called a truce.

I simply said, "Apology accepted." I was never one to hold grudges. Grudges only kept the grudge-holder in bondage, and I didn't want that.

"Good night, then, Miss Talbot," he said and walked away.

I packed up the last of the leftovers from lunch and placed them into my picnic basket. Without a refrigerator, the food wouldn't survive until the next day, so I decided to take it home to my family. I caught a cab to the water taxi and soon found my way home to Governor's Harbour. It had been a long, interesting day and I couldn't wait to see what tomorrow had in store. Couldn't wait to see if Jackson Conner would surprise me again. Wondered if he'd have a kind word or a nice gesture. It was certainly something to look forward to.

Chapter 7

Jasmine

The waves of the ocean crashed against the shore. Palm trees swayed in the wind, and a little bird rested on the wooden banister of the porch just a few feet away. I looked up from my computer and took in the beauty and captivating view that the back side of the house had to offer. It was by far one of the best views on the island. And once construction had been completed and the back porch restored, I knew that it would be the most coveted place on the property. It was getting late and the sun was beginning to set—my favorite time of the day. It was the sign of completion—the end of one day in preparation for another.

I had been there all day, working on our marketing plan. Books were spread out all over the place and my computer was resting in my lap, and my pink earbuds were in my ear. As I'd listened to Jah Cure and allowed him to tease my senses with his smooth Caribbean rhythms, I'd lost track of time. Now I took a deep breath, inhaling the fresh smell of the ocean, and then rested my head against the beach towel that I'd spread over the back of an old wooden lounger. I was winding down, and my eyes were tired from staring at the screen all day. I figured it was time I headed for the water taxi, before I fell asleep right there.

I packed up my belongings and walked toward the house. The sound of hammering had me frozen for a moment. It was odd because I was sure that Jackson and his men had wrapped things up for the day. A few of the men had long ago poked their heads out back and wished me a good night. The noise ceased, and then I heard something that sounded like sanding.

"Hello!" I yelled. When I got no answer I followed the noise; it was coming from upstairs. I stood at the foot of the stairs and called out again. "Hello. Who's there?"

Jackson appeared at the top of the stairs, wearing a pair of black Levi's, work boots and no shirt. His bare chest had me mesmerized for a moment. His golden body was moist from the sweat, his abs tight, his chest a mountain of steel and his shoulders broad. Looking at him, I lost my train of thought.

"It's me," he said.

"I didn't know anyone else was here."

"Yeah, you seemed so comfortable back there on the porch…I didn't want to bother you. I'm still working up here."

He walked away, disappearing into one of the rooms.

I climbed the stairs to see what Jackson was up to. I followed him into my future office. The walls had been painted in hues of red and orange, and the desk that I'd spotted in the storage shed rested in the center of the room. Jackson was sanding the desk.

"What are you doing?" I asked, although it was obvious what he was up to.

"I wanted to have this completely sanded by the time you got here in the morning."

"And the room…" I looked around at the walls. "…you painted it."

"Yeah, I did."

"How did you know what color I wanted? You didn't even bother to ask me."

"I just took a wild guess. You mentioned that you liked bright colors…so I just went with that. If you don't like it, I can have it repainted."

"No, it'll do," I said. I didn't want him to know that I absolutely adored the colors.

"I'll have the wood finished on your desk by tomorrow."

"What color?"

"Dark walnut," he said. "Is that okay?"

"That's fine," I said. "I really appreciate you doing this. It means a lot."

"My pleasure."

"How's your stomach today?"

"Huh? Oh, much better. Thank you for the lemon water. It worked very well."

"Glad to hear it. You get stomachaches often?"

"Only when I drink more than I should," he admitted and then looked as if he hadn't meant to share so much. "I went out drinking with my guys the other night. Overextended myself. A stupid thing to do when you're recovering from a stomach ulcer."

"Yeah, that was pretty stupid. How long have you had an ulcer?"

"Since law school. It hasn't recurred since then, but I'm careful about doing the right things. No spicy foods, no heavy drinking. I usually stay away from the triggers."

"Except the other night." I smiled.

When he smiled in return his whole face lit up. "Exactly."

"Well, I'm glad you're feeling better." I wanted to touch those muscles. See how firm they were. Instead, I reached my hand out for a shake. "Well, thank you for having the room painted so quickly. And for sanding the desk."

He took my hand in his. His hands were rugged, not soft and gentle. I imagined them caressing my body. It had been so long since I'd felt the touch of a man, and I immediately longed for it.

"Why don't you stick around for a bit? Help me paint the desk," he said.

"I'm not really dressed for painting."

"I have an extra old T-shirt in my bag."

Before I could answer, he'd already pulled the shirt out of his bag and tossed it to me. "Put that on."

I gave him a look that said, *There you go acting like my daddy again...trying to tell me what to do.* He caught the look.

"Don't get your panties in a wad," he said. He smiled a beautiful wide grin, showing a nice set of white teeth. "I'm asking, not telling. Please can you change into my shirt and help me paint *your* desk?"

"Sure." I smiled a flirty smile and then went into the bathroom across the hall.

I checked my hair in the mirror, making sure I wasn't looking out of sorts. I smelled his shirt to see if it had been worn recently. It smelled of fabric softener. I pulled it over my head. It was a professional basketball T-shirt, black with the player's name sprawled across the back in bold white letters. I walked back into the room where Jackson had started to sand the desk again.

"That's better," he said, looking up at me.

"You know, I really shouldn't wear this shirt."

"Why?"

"I'm really not feeling this guy right now." I was refer-ring to the player whose shirt I wore. "I read somewhere that he cheated on his woman. He's not a man of honor."

"That may be but he's a great ballplayer, though," Jack-son said. "And for that reason, you should wear that shirt with pride. Who cares about what he does in his personal life?"

"I care."

"People get too caught up in that stuff."

"I used to see him all the time in downtown LA. Some-times with his girlfriend," I explained. "I liked him once upon a time. Hard to believe he's a filthy cheater now."

"Whoa! You're prejudging the man. You don't know the details or the circumstances surrounding his infidel-ity. And besides…he ain't married!"

"But he's in a committed relationship. Doesn't that mean anything anymore?"

"It means everything to some men. But we're talking about a professional ballplayer."

"So because he's a pro ballplayer, he gets a pass?"

"I'm not saying that," he explained as he handed me a sand block.

I began sanding the opposite side of the desk. "Then what are you saying?"

"I'm simply saying that ballplayers are…I don't know… expected to cheat. I mean…the pressures of being famous have to be tough. And you have women throwing it at them from every possible angle. What's a man to do?"

"Throw it back!" My Bahamian accent was much stron-ger when I got heated.

He laughed. A deep, hearty laugh. "Throw it back?" He

kept laughing, mocking my accent, and soon I began laughing, too. It was the first good laugh I'd had in some time.

Jackson and I spent the next several minutes talking about every team in the NBA. He discussed the players and the dynamics of the game while I talked about their personal lives—the types of cars they drove, whom they were dating and how often I'd seen them wandering about LA. By the time we were done, I had changed my opinion about Jackson. I actually liked him. He was not at all what I'd expected.

"You're very beautiful. And witty. And bright." He said it out of the clear blue.

It was an uneasy moment, when a man actually looked at me square in the eyes and called me beautiful. Men raved about my beauty all the time, but this was different. And never had I been called witty. The only affirmations I'd received from any man in my life had come from my father, so it was definitely an unexpected treat.

"Thank you," I whispered.

"You're not at all what I'd expected," he said.

Funny. I'd just thought the same thing about him. "What were you expecting?"

"I knew you'd be beautiful, but I didn't expect you to have a sense of humor, or that you'd be…I don't know… smart."

"You didn't expect me to be smart?"

"I was expecting this Valley girl with the mirrored shades and the funky attitude. Snooty and clueless. I prejudged you."

"Yes, you did, sir. You've been watching too much television. Women from California are not all Valley girls. Bright professional women hail from the Golden State, too." I took a bow.

"It's just that you went to Spelman and studied…what?"

"Economics. With a minor in sociology."

"I never would've guessed that. Why didn't you go work for one of those major companies in Atlanta after college?"

"I had other dreams to pursue," I admitted, although my admission only made me feel small and as *clueless* as he described earlier.

I remembered my graduation and feeling overwhelmed with the thoughts of pursuing a career in economics. I wasn't sure of myself. Wasn't sure that I'd survive in a large corporation where the competition was tough, and people stepped on you and threw you under the bus, just so they could advance their own careers. I'd seen my older brother and sister conquer the world, and I'd seen their wounds. Edward had been dragged through the mud on the campaign trail. His marriage to his high school sweetheart had ended in divorce because he'd invested too much time preparing for office and not enough time being a husband and father to his five-year-old daughter.

And Alyson had built a successful career as a real-estate professional, selling million-dollar homes to rich celebrities all over the Bahamas—in Nassau, Freeport and Eleuthera. But she was unhappy. Alyson had been determined not to follow in the footsteps of our mother, who had sacrificed her teaching career to follow my father to the Bahamas. No, Alyson would never do that. She was bound to pursue her dreams no matter what, and she wouldn't give them up for any man, nor spend the rest of her life having babies. Alyson wasn't interested in love or children.

It was me who wanted children—as many as the grains of sand along the Caribbean Sea—and marriage to a man just like my father. We'd live in a beautiful, simple little house on the Eleuthera Islands, just like my grandparents and my parents did. Free-spirited and outgoing, I didn't want to be held captive by corporate America, tired and frustrated all the time, never able to enjoy life.

"What about you?" I asked Jackson. "Why did you drop out of Harvard?"

"Did I tell you that I dropped out of Harvard?"

"People talk," I said.

"It's a long, boring story. You wouldn't be interested in hearing it," he said.

"No, I really would like to hear it."

I tried standing from the position I was squatting in, but I stumbled and almost fell. Jackson grabbed me, his hands holding on to my waist. My eyes met his as he looked down at me. His six-foot frame towered over me, my chin just about at his chest. He pulled me closer. Close enough that I smelled just a hint of his cologne; it had worn off through the course of the day. My heart beat a little faster, and my hormones stirred. I suddenly wanted his lips against mine. There was no mistaking it was what he wanted, too. Pulling me close was no accident. His nose touched mine as if he were contemplating a kiss. If he didn't do it soon, I was going to do it for him. And then his lips lightly brushed against mine.

"Hello!" a voice yelled from downstairs. "Anybody here?"

"Daddy?" I whispered.

"Is that your father?" asked Jackson.

I pulled away from Jackson and walked out of the office. "Daddy, I'm up here!"

I was nervous for some reason. I felt as if I were an adolescent and my father had caught me with a boy in my room again. Like the time Darren had climbed through my window and spent the night on my bedroom floor wrapped in my grandmother's quilt. I'd forgotten to awaken him before morning. My parents and his were outraged. It changed the relationship between the two families. My father wanted to shoot him; his parents thought me to be a jezebel. It was odd that my father had been the one to awaken me for school that morning. Alyson was usually the one assigned to awaken Whitney and me for school. It was as though she'd known that Darren was there and had sent my parents in to witness it with their own eyes.

I went to the top of the stairwell. "Daddy, what are you doing here?"

"Well, I waited for you at the water taxi and you never showed up. Called your cell phone and you didn't answer."

"Oh, I'm sorry, Dad. I meant to call." I searched my back pockets for my phone and then realized I'd left it in the bathroom when I'd changed into Jackson's shirt.

"Hello, Mr. Talbot." Jackson appeared behind me. I was grateful that he'd thought to cover his shirtless torso. He rushed down the stairs to give my father a proper handshake. "I've heard a lot about you from your son Edward. A pleasure to finally meet you, sir."

"Jackson, right?" asked my father, who was obviously trying to piece together why his daughter had been upstairs in an unfinished house with a strange man.

"Yes, sir. Jackson Conner."

My father scratched his head, gave a look that I wasn't quite able to read. "How's the renovation coming along, Mr. Conner?"

"Call me Jackson, please. And things are moving well. We haven't had any bumps in the road just yet."

"That's good to hear," said my dad. "I see you've become acquainted with my lovely daughter."

"Yes, sir. We've created her an office upstairs—a place where she can work while on the property. She found an old desk in the storage shed, and we were busy sanding it…and…"

"Her office?"

"Yes, Daddy. My office. I need an office," I interjected.

"Of course, you need an office." My father held his

hands up in surrender. "So, would you like a ride home or were you planning to continue...*sanding*?"

"I'll get my things." I went into the bathroom and grabbed my phone, my laptop and other belongings, then made my way downstairs. I turned to Jackson. "Thank you for painting the room. And for the desk."

"No problem," he said.

"I'll see you tomorrow, then."

"Good night, Jasmine," said Jackson. "Nice meeting you, sir."

Daddy bade Jackson a farewell and then grabbed my laptop bag from my shoulder. The two of us made the short journey to the water taxi.

As Daddy maneuvered the pickup down Queen's Highway, I stared out the window. Thoughts of Jackson filled my head, and I wondered what might have happened had Daddy not shown up so suddenly. I wondered what Jackson's kiss might've tasted like and what his arms might've felt like had he had the opportunity to wrap them around me.

"You okay?" asked Daddy.

"Fine."

With a nod and a half smile, he looked ahead. "Seems like you have a lot on your mind."

"Just thinking about the Grove."

"I see. It's a complicated project, the Grove is. Isn't it?"

"Yeah, I guess so."

"I'm sure it has you thrown off guard a bit. Projects like this tend to make us rethink everything in our lives, and the interesting thing is, they only come around once in a blue moon."

"Are we still talking about the Grove?" I asked.

"Of course," Daddy said. "What did you think we were talking about?"

"The Grove," I mumbled and gave my father a sideways glance.

He grinned and then began to hum along with the old Caribbean song that played on the radio in his truck.

Chapter 8

Jackson

I found some contemporary jazz on my iPhone and continued to work until I had Jasmine's desk completely sanded. I brushed my hand across the smoothness of it and felt a sense of pride. It felt good to do something nice for her. I was feeling strange things for a woman who had gotten under my skin just days before. As much as I hated to admit it, she'd awakened things inside of me. More often than I cared to remember, I thought of her long after I left the Grove some evenings. I wondered what she was up to—and if she thought of me, too.

Fitting her into my world didn't seem feasible or practical. We were too different. Our priorities were as far apart as the continents. Our lives were far from parallel, and I couldn't think of one thing we had in common—other than the Grove. We both loved that place.

I loved watching her walk, and I adored her smile. Her eyes were intoxicating, and her curves stirred my senses.

I spread the first coat of dark walnut onto the sanded desk. Then I rested on the floor with my back against the wall as the stain dried and thought of Jasmine Talbot. I wanted her. I was man enough to admit that—even if I admitted it to only myself.

I wanted to wrap her brown legs around my waist and kiss her sexy lips. I wanted to make her feel things between her thighs that she'd never felt before. I wanted to nibble on her round breasts and drive her crazy with the dancing of my fingertips. The chemistry between us was undeniable, although I'd tried hard to deny mine.

I began to clean up my mess, wash paintbrushes and pack up my toolbox. I left the Grove feeling a sense of accomplishment. I'd managed to put a smile on Jasmine Talbot's face, and she had done the same to mine. And I had fully intended to finish whatever it was we'd started, but maybe her father's interruption was a sign. A sign that I needed to refocus my energy. I'd allowed my physical attraction for her to get in the way of my good sense. And the last thing I wanted to do was make the Grove awkward for either of us. We shared a business relationship, and that was all.

Back at my hotel, I took a long shower and tried to wash away any thoughts of Jasmine. It was foolish to think that anything would come of this. Neither of us was looking for romance—at least I wasn't. I already had my hands full with work, and that was my priority.

I don't know what made me do an online search for phone records of Eleutheran residents. Who knew there was actually a telephone directory that listed every Island resident by name? I went straight to the *T*s and searched for the Talbots. With my finger skimming carefully across the computer screen, I located the name of Paul John Talbot—Jasmine's father.

I contemplated calling the house. Perhaps Jasmine would answer and I wouldn't have to go through the formalities and the embarrassment of asking to speak to her. I could pretend to talk business, ask her about her visions for the Grove. But the truth was, I needed to hear her voice.

Why don't you just call her brother Edward and ask for her cell number? My inner voice never seemed to know when to shut up. It constantly got me into the silliest of predicaments.

I called the house instead.

"Hello," a woman's sweet voice answered.

"Hello. Is this the Talbot home?"

"Yes, it is."

What do you say now, genius?

"This is Jackson Conner. I'm the contractor for the Grove. I'm a friend of Edward's from college. Is this Mrs. Talbot?"

"Yes, it is!" Her voice seemed to smile. "And how are you, Mr. Conner? Edward has told us so much about you. We can't wait to meet you."

"Likewise, ma'am."

"Well now, it's good you called. I was going to invite you to dinner this Saturday. Are you free?"

"Yes, ma'am, I am."

"Good, then. I'll have Paul John pick you up at your hotel. Where are you staying?" she asked.

"At the Coral Sands. But I wouldn't want to put Mr. Talbot to any trouble. I can find my way."

"It's no trouble at all."

"Thank you, but I can manage. I'm really quite the navigator," I told her.

"Okay, baby. Four o'clock, then."

"I'll be there."

"Good! Was there something else you needed, honey? Did you call to talk to Paul?"

No, I really called to talk to your beautiful daughter. Wanted her to know that she's turned my world upside down. Got me behaving like Dr. Jekyll and Mr. Hyde. I don't even know why I'm on the other end of this phone with you right now.

"No, ma'am. I just called to say hello and introduce myself. I promised Edward I'd get over there to visit with you and Mr. Talbot."

"Well, good. Saturday's perfect."

"What can I bring?"

"You bring yourself and an appetite. That's it."

"I'm already looking forward to it."

I hung up and then stood there for a moment trying to make sense of what had just happened. I thought I was losing my mind, calling the Talbots' home like a young schoolboy. Had Jasmine answered, I'd have been at a loss for words. And what about Mr. Talbot? Surely he knew that Jasmine and I were doing more upstairs than sanding her desk. I'd have done better calling Edward for Jasmine's cell number, but then I wouldn't have dinner plans for Saturday night.

Chapter 9

Jasmine

The house smelled of Caribbean spices. Calypso and goombay sounds played on my father's old record player. My parents loved the old-school sounds of George Symonette and played his albums only on special occasions. Which was strange because it was just an ordinary Saturday. In fact, I had just completed my ordinary Saturday afternoon errands and shopping at the Market Place Shopping Centre in Rock Sound. Denny wore his Sunday shirt, khakis and loafers, a change from his usual graphic T-shirts, denim shorts and flip-flops. I knew something was up.

"What's going on?" I asked him. "Why are they playing George Symonette, and why are you wearing khakis?"

"Someone's coming for dinner."

"Who?"

"That contractor fellow," said Denny as he placed my

mother's antique dinnerware on the table. "Edward's friend. The one they hired to do the construction at the Grove."

"Are you kidding?" I asked.

"Not at all. He'll be here in an hour," he said. "Ma wants you to get changed and help her in the kitchen."

"Why do they have to be so…so…cordial?"

"They entertain all the time. What's the big deal?" asked Denny.

It was true. My parents had always entertained people in our home for as long as I could remember. They were friendly and welcoming, a trait of most Bahamians—especially when people visited the island from the US. They made a point of introducing them to the traditional tastes of the islands. So I wasn't surprised that they'd invited Jackson over for dinner, but I would've liked a heads-up.

"It's just that it's a regular old Saturday," I tried explaining to Denny.

"Well, Saturday or not, he's coming. And I think they invited him to sleep over."

This was getting worse by the minute.

"How do you know that?"

"Ma just put fresh sheets on Edward's old bed."

I groaned and then rushed down the hall to my bedroom. I needed to check my hair and find something subtly sexy to wear, and I didn't have much time. As I searched my closet for an outfit, I heard a light tap on the door.

"Jazzy." I heard my mother's voice on the other side of the door before she opened it. "Come on into the kitchen. I need you to cut up the vegetables for the conch salad and I need you to prepare the batter for the johnny cakes."

I was no stranger to the kitchen. My mother made sure my sisters and I knew how to cook. She taught us how to prepare every Caribbean dish imaginable from pigeon peas and rice to conch fritters. Although my mother wasn't from the Bahamas, my grandmother had taught her everything she knew about the native dishes. Over the years she'd even picked up the native tongue, her Bahamian accent just as strong as those who were born and raised on the island.

"I was just about to hop in the shower," I told her.

"It can wait, child. Mr. Conner will be here shortly."

She didn't give me a chance to object. Instead she shut the door. With my father, there was always room for negotiation. But Beverly Talbot didn't negotiate with her children.

Reluctantly I limited myself to pulling my hair into a ponytail and refreshing my lip gloss. Then I joined my mother in the kitchen and grabbed an apron from the pantry.

She chopped the conch fish into small pieces for the salad and then pulled the baked grouper out of the oven. She stopped for a moment and shook her booty to the Caribbean rhythm, and then she took a sip of her sky juice—a mixture of fresh coconut water, sweet milk and gin. She barely drank, except for special occasions. She grabbed my hands and forced me to dance with her. Calypso wasn't my style of music, but it was definitely familiar. We were a musical family.

"What's on your mind, Jazzy?" my mother asked.

"Nothing really."

"Your father tells me that you've already bumped heads with this young man, Jackson Conner. What's your trouble with him?"

"He's just a bit arrogant and cocky. That's all." That was my old opinion of Jackson. I'd since changed what I thought of him.

"And he's very handsome, I hear," she said, raising an eyebrow.

"And who on earth would've told you that?" I asked.

"This is a small island, sugar. And people talk," said

Mama as she walked over and stirred the pot filled with steamed cabbage.

"He's not hard on the eyes, but his ego is bigger than the island."

"You must be referring to Jackson Conner." I heard my sister's all-too-familiar voice. "Hey, Jasmine."

"Alyson. What are you doing here?" I asked.

"Besides the fact that this is my family's home and I have an open invitation to come here as often as I want," she said, "I was invited for the weekend."

I glanced at my mother, who gave me a wicked smile. It was obvious that she was playing matchmaker, and I didn't like it one bit. I didn't necessarily have dibs on Jackson, but I didn't want anyone else to either. Not before I had the opportunity to tread those waters myself.

"Well, it's good to see you," I lied as I gave my sister a tight squeeze. I couldn't remember the last time I was happy to see her. She made my life a living hell every time we entered into the same space. "When did you get here?"

"Daddy just picked me up from Governor's Harbour Airport."

"You look fabulous!" my mother raved. "You'll have to share your secrets for slimming down. I could stand to lose a few pounds myself."

"I don't mind sharing with you, Ma," said Alyson. "Everybody can't look like Jasmine. Some of us have to work hard and make sacrifices for the things we want."

I rolled my eyes at my sister. I knew her comment wasn't about weight at all. She looked wonderful, but her attitude was still the same and I wasn't up for a challenge with her. I had my own issues. In just a short time, Jackson Conner would be in this house and that was too much sexual energy for anyone to deal with. It had been only two days since our awkward *almost-kiss*. No doubt, there was something between us, but I wasn't sure if I was ready to figure out what it was or deal with the emotional ramifications of it over dinner with the entire family. I'd had enough heartache to last me a lifetime. In California, I'd rushed into a whirlwind relationship with my agent. I'd simply been one of his many client-turned-girlfriends. And when he became bored with me, he moved on to his next pursuit. I didn't need a repeat of that.

It seemed to be the story of my life. I attracted men who wanted a nice lay, but who didn't take the time to get to know me—*the real me*. It cost me many tears and many hours of therapy, trying to understand what was wrong with me. Why I couldn't attract a decent man who would love me for me. The answer was simple. I hadn't loved myself enough for someone else to do the same. I hadn't taken the time to know the real me, so how could I expect someone else to do it? Being home had given me such freedom.

"I'm gonna go get settled into my old room," said Alyson, her overnight bag draped over her shoulder. "I'll change and help out in the kitchen."

"No need," Mom said. "Jasmine and I can handle it. Go freshen up for dinner."

Kissing my forehead as he entered the kitchen, Daddy said, "Our dinner guest is here."

Suddenly, my heart pounded rapidly.

"He's early," said Mama. "We're not quite ready yet."

"It's okay. I'll entertain him on the porch for a while." Daddy grabbed two bottles of Bahamian Sands beer from the refrigerator. "Holler when you're ready."

I wanted to rush to the porch and sneak a peek at Jackson. I wondered what he looked like when he wasn't barking orders to his men on the construction site. Wanted to know what type of clothes he wore to family dinners. Yesterday, I'd purposely kept away from the Grove altogether, opting to work at home instead. I wanted to avoid all interactions with Jackson until I had time to absorb our last encounter. I had analyzed every touch, every glance and every word we'd spoken.

"Let's get this food on the table, Jazzy," my mother said, breaking into my thoughts. She began putting food into serving dishes and ushered me to assist. I had no further time to think about Jackson or how he'd look.

Dressed in a white button-down shirt with gray casual slacks and loafers, Jackson looked as if he'd just stepped from the pages of *GQ* magazine. With a curly head of hair and his skin as smooth as a baby's, he was hard not to look at. I forced myself not to stare, even though I wanted to study him. His cologne lingered in the air as he walked past me to take the seat directly across from me at the table. If his goal was to torture me through dinner, to make me feel uncomfortable, he was definitely off to a good start.

"Good to see you again, Jasmine," he said.

"Likewise."

"And this is my daughter Alyson," said Mama.

Alyson stepped into the dining room. She wore a conservative light blue sundress with a cropped denim jacket draped over it. Her hair brushed freely against her shoulders, and, surprisingly, she wore eyeshadow and lipstick. Makeup was a rarity for her, but for some reason she'd chosen to wear it to dinner. For Jackson? As much as I hated to admit it, she looked beautiful. All of the Talbot women were beautiful in their own natural sort of way.

She took the empty seat next to Jackson. "So, Jackson, I understand you're from Key West." She didn't waste any time jumping into questions.

"Yes. Born and raised there."

"Is your family from the islands at all?" she asked.

"No, my parents are from Louisiana originally. They moved to Florida long before I was born."

"That's a rarity. A black family migrating to Key West from somewhere other than the Bahamas. And from Louisiana, of all places. Oooh." She frowned.

"What's wrong with Louisiana?" Jackson asked.

"Nothing. It's just so…" She paused for a second. "…it's just unheard of, that's all."

She always tried to be an authority on everything.

"It's really not so rare." Jackson set her straight. "People migrate from all over."

"I too grew up in the Keys," Daddy said. "My wife and I followed my parents here after they retired."

"I live in Old Town. I refurbished a little two-story historic conch house there a few years ago."

"I'd like to see Old Town again. I bet it's changed quite a bit since the last time I was there."

"When were you last there?" asked Jackson.

"Oh, about twenty years ago," Daddy explained. "Once I started my medical practice here, it was almost impossible to leave the island for any amount of time. Doctors are rare in the Bahamas—almost nonexistent when I came over. I was virtually on call twenty-four hours a day before I retired."

"Is your wife from the Bahamas also?"

"No, my mother is not Bahamian," Alyson interjected, as if the question had been posed to her. "You must've noticed that her accent is not as strong."

"I think her accent is just as strong as most islanders," I said.

"My wife is from Washington, DC." Daddy smiled at my mother. "Although she's not from the Bahamas originally, she's an island girl now."

"I am definitely an island girl now." Mama smiled back at Daddy.

"We moved here when my father took sick. I wanted to be near him before his death. All of our children were born here, with the exception of Edward, who was born in Old Town just like you. So the two of you have more in common than you probably knew." My father loaded his plate with another piece of fish and two more johnny cakes.

My mother gave him a cross-eyed look. "Easy on the johnny cakes, mister. Remember, you're watching your cholesterol."

"Yes, Daddy, I'll be watching you this weekend. Every morsel that you eat," Alyson said.

My father ignored the comments from both of them and continued with Jackson. "Edward tells me the two of you met at Harvard Law School."

"Yes, sir, we did. We became friends very quickly. Your son is a good man." Jackson filled his mouth with cabbage, carefully avoiding the small pile of pigeon peas and rice on his plate. He'd obviously placed it there out of courtesy to the cook.

"Don't like pigeon peas and rice?" I asked, watching him way too close.

"Actually I've never tried them before." Jackson smiled at me.

"They're very good," Mama said to Jackson, "but my feelings won't be hurt if you don't like them."

He took a forkful of them and chewed slowly, then laid his fork down and wiped his mouth with his napkin. He took a long drink of ice water.

"He doesn't like them," I said before stuffing a forkful of cabbage into my mouth.

"Sit up straight in your chair, Jazzy," my mother tried whispering but all too loudly. All eyes landed on me.

I was instantly embarrassed and told her so with the look I gave her. Although I was slouching a bit, I wondered why she felt the need to bring it to everyone's attention— particularly when the man who made my heart flutter was seated right across from me at the table.

"I'm sorry. I'm not too keen on the pigeon peas and rice." Jackson smiled at my mother apologetically. "But the fish and cabbage is delicious. And I love the johnny cakes."

"Jasmine cooked the johnny cakes." Daddy smiled and gave me a wink.

"Yes, she did," my mother concurred. "Jasmine is a very good cook. Alyson, too."

"The johnny cakes are delicious, Jasmine." Jackson captured my eyes for a moment and I stared back.

I took in his handsome features. His face wasn't clean-shaven at all. It was a bit rugged and there was a faint bit of stubble that covered his cheeks and rested on his chin. His eyes were gentle and his smile genuine.

"Thank you," I managed to say before looking away, embarrassed that I'd stared so long.

"Jackson, please help yourself to the food, and don't hesitate to make yourself at home. After dinner, Alyson will show you to Edward's old bedroom and maybe the two of you could take a stroll after the sun sets." My mother smiled.

"Thank you, Mrs. Talbot. I really appreciate dinner. A home-cooked meal is so much better than eating at the local hotels. And your hospitality is undeniable. Thank you."

My mother looked at Jackson, set her fork down onto her plate. "What's your mother like? She taught you the best of manners."

"My mother is a very strong woman. She's very assertive and doesn't fit into anybody's mold. Not afraid to speak her mind."

Alyson laughed. "She sounds a lot like me. She and I would probably fare very well together."

"Hmm. I don't know. Probably not," said Jackson. "My experience has been that women who are too much alike have a hard time getting along."

"Your experience with women has brought you to this conclusion?" Alyson asked.

"My experience with life," he said as he gave Alyson a gentle smile.

I laughed inside. Did he just *dis* her?

Denny, who had been unusually quiet during dinner, asked to be excused from the table. After my father excused him, Denny stood and held his hand out to Jackson and said, "It was good meeting you, Jackson."

Jackson stood, took Denny's hand in a firm shake. "Good meeting you, too, Denny. And if I don't see you before you leave for the Royal Bahamas, good luck on your tour of duty."

"Thanks."

Denny rushed from the table and into his room. When he came out, he'd changed out of his dinner garb and into a pair of cargo shorts, an old T-shirt and flip-flops. He dashed out the back door, no doubt taking the back route to Sage's house. It seemed that the two of them spent every waking hour together, not wanting to waste a single moment before his deployment. He couldn't wait to get away and I found myself wishing I had somewhere to get away to myself.

After dessert, Jackson and Alyson took a walk through our neighborhood, as my mother had suggested. Mama kept herself busy in the kitchen, while my father and I retired to the front porch.

"Your mother has a bad habit of playing matchmaker," Daddy said as he took a sip from his beer.

"Yeah, she does," I had to agree.

"For what it's worth, he's no more interested in Alyson than I'm interested in watching my cholesterol." He smiled.

"That's not a good analogy, Daddy. You need to be interested in your cholesterol." I looked at my father. "And I don't care whether or not he's interested in her."

"Really? Is that why you kept your nose buried in your plate all through dinner?"

"I talked…about some stuff…" I muttered.

"I barely even knew you were there."

"She deserves love."

"Yes, but not with Jackson. Particularly since he has eyes for someone else." My father was very intuitive.

"Who?" I blushed.

"Stevie Wonder could see that he has eyes for you," he roared with laughter. "Why are you so hesitant, Jazzy?"

"What do you mean?"

"I know you're not shy, child. Your old dad has eyes. Why aren't you going for what you want?"

"Too many bad relationships."

"Love is a funny thing sometimes. We get in and out of relationships with people we don't even like, much less love. And then we're not able to recognize when the real thing comes along." He laughed a bit. "Isn't it funny?"

"Yep," I said, "but you've never had to worry about that. You and Ma have been in love since the beginning of time."

"Yeah, but I've met a lot of people who have missed out on the loves of their lives because they didn't recognize it when it stared them in the face."

In the shade on the front porch, my father and I talked about life and relationships. I missed times like these with him. When I was younger, we'd sit on the porch for hours and analyze things. He filled my head with our family's history, telling stories of the old days. Although I was very young when my grandparents passed away, I felt as if I knew them well. My father made sure they never left my heart.

Before long, Jackson and Alyson returned from their walk. As they sauntered toward the house, Alyson laughed and played with her hair—a true indication that she was attracted to Jackson. I frowned.

"I'm going for my run," I announced and then stood quickly.

"Aren't you the least bit interested in hearing what transpired on that walk?" he asked.

"Not even the least bit." I gave my father a kiss on the cheek. "Good night, Daddy. I love you."

"Night, sweetheart. Love you, too."

Chapter 10

Jasmine

I changed into a pair of running pants—the ones that hugged my butt in all the right places—and a cropped running top that revealed my toned abs. I pulled my hair back into a ponytail and slipped on my sneakers. I needed to get a run in before the sun had completely set along the ocean. With my headphones wrapped around my neck and my iPhone tuned to my Caribbean playlist, I went into the kitchen to fill my water bottle.

"You're a runner." It was more a statement, not a question.

I turned to find that Jackson had changed into a pair of knee-length basketball shorts, a Bob Marley T-shirt and a pair of Nike slides.

"Yes, I am."

"Mind if I join you?" he asked.

"You run?"

"Is that so hard to believe?" he asked and then flashed a beautiful smile. "I've been known to run a couple hundred…feet."

We both laughed.

"You plan to run in that?" I asked.

Jackson looked down at his clothing and shrugged. "Yeah."

"Well, come on, then."

"I'll grab my sneakers," he said and rushed out of the kitchen.

I stood over the sink and filled my bottle with tap water. When I turned around I was staring my sister in the eyes.

"Going for a run, Jasmine?"

"Yep." Alyson was a master at twisting my words and enticing me into confrontation and I wasn't up for that right now. I twisted the cap onto my water bottle and took a drink.

"I'm ready," said Jackson as he entered the kitchen.

"Oh, the two of you are going for a run together."

"She's going to show me how this is done," Jackson teased.

We dashed out the back door before Alyson could ask any more questions. We walked a few feet until we reached the beach, and then I started to jog in place.

"Ready?" I asked.

"I guess," Jackson laughed.

I began at a slow pace just so that he could keep up.

"What's the deal with your sister?" he asked. "Why is she so tightly wired?"

"Hmm. That's a different way of describing Alyson." I smiled. "Didn't you enjoy your walk with her?"

"We mostly talked business. She gave me her expectations for the renovation of the Grove," he said. "She has a lot of opinions about you, too."

"I just bet she does," I said. "Alyson lives in her own perfect world, and no one can live up to her expectations. Especially me."

"Why not you?"

"She's always had this thing with me. Treats me as if I don't know what I'm doing in life. Like I'm incapable of making decisions. She thinks I can't handle the Grove. She and Edward wanted to hire someone to write our business and marketing plan, when I'm fully capable of doing it."

"Have you ever written a business or marketing plan?"

"Not officially, but I can do it."

He raised one eyebrow as he looked at me. "Are you the problem child in the family?"

"I think that a couple of my siblings probably believe that I am, because I didn't follow their blueprint for my life. I don't know what my brother told you about me, but I'm not clueless and I'm not living off my parents. I'm here because I was the only one who volunteered to move back home and take over the Grove. I had plenty of offers from major corporations after college, but I went to California to pursue my dreams first."

"What are your dreams?"

"I wanted to be an actress. Wish I'd gone to an arts school and studied drama. I landed a few minor roles and a few modeling gigs, too."

Jackson smiled.

"Why are you smiling?"

"Why wouldn't you secure your future first, and then go chasing after your dreams?"

"Don't judge me. You sound like them. And what authority do you have to tell anyone when they should chase after their dreams?"

"I'm not judging you. We all have dreams, but dreams don't pay the bills or put food on the table."

"I'm not a practical girl. I don't function well in a nine-to-five type of environment. I need freedom."

"It's who you are. I get that, but now you're asking them to give you a chance to pull off something practical, when you're not a practical person."

"I'm not practical, but I usually have a plan for things," I told Jackson. "It's true, I've made some bad decisions, but I've learned from my mistakes. So why should I continue to be judged for them? And why does the harshest judgment come from people who love you the most?"

With a somber look on his face, Jackson turned his head. It was as if I'd hit a nerve.

"What?" I asked.

"You're right," he finally said. "Maybe the Grove is just what you need to earn your family's trust."

"I know it is. But I don't need their approval. The Grove is my inheritance, too. And I've never been more committed to anything in my life."

He nodded and we jogged farther down the beach. He struggled to keep up.

"You need to rest?" I asked.

"Can we?"

"Sure."

We stopped running for a moment.

Jackson bent over to catch his breath and then stood. "How often do you work out?"

"I try to do something every day…whether it be running or yoga. Sometimes I lift weights with my brother. What about you? Do you work out at all?"

"Not as often as I should," Jackson said. "I don't have a lot of time to do anything but work. My friends and family call me a workaholic."

"They're probably right."

"Guilty as charged." He raised his hand like a Boy Scout. "I notice you have your headphones around your neck. What's on your playlist?"

"Jah Cure, Beres Hammond. Caribbean artists that you're probably not familiar with."

He pulled on the hem of his Marley T-shirt with both hands. "I know Bob Marley," he said.

"Good for you." I smiled. "Marley's cool."

"Let me hear some of your music," he said. "What's your favorite song?"

I sorted through my playlist and found my favorite Jah Cure tune—a ballad about unconditional love. I turned up the volume as loud as it would go. The waves of the ocean seemed to crash against the shore in perfect rhythm with the music. As Jackson listened intently to the words, I took a drink from my water bottle and then set it down.

"Let me hear it again," he said.

I went back to the track and played it again. I started moving my hips in a circular motion, my eyes closed, one hand in the air and an arm around my waist. I got lost in the music. When I opened my eyes, Jackson was watching, studying me. I grabbed his hand and encouraged him to dance with me. He moved a little.

He grabbed my waist with both hands. Much like he had the night of our *almost-kiss*. His body pressed against mine, we danced to the Caribbean beat. With a quick twirl, my back relaxed against him. His arms wrapped tightly around me from behind, I rested my head against his chest. Still moving. Still swaying. My hormones began to rage and I couldn't think of one place I'd rather have been than right there. He planted sweet kisses along the back of my neck, and when I turned to face him he planted those same kisses onto my forehead and nose. Soon his lips found mine, and this time without interruption. His kiss was gentle, and his tongue found its way between my lips and danced with my tongue. I savored the taste of him. The bulge that I felt against my belly, I wanted to feel in other places. I wanted to caress him there, but I fought the urge.

"You're so damn beautiful," he whispered.

I moved my hands along his chest and took his face, caressing it gently. "We should continue our run," I said.

"You think so?" he asked, holding me tighter.

"I think so."

I was certain that if we didn't continue our run, we'd end up rolling about in the sand and I'd be filled with regrets. Too often, I'd gotten caught up in the moment and made rash decisions.

Lately I'd been contemplating exactly what it was I had to offer. Beauty was a given, and I had successfully chiseled the perfect body. But I wanted to be respected for more than that. I wanted my siblings to see my worth. I wanted the next man who came into my life to receive the full package. For a person who had sold herself short for so long, I had to dig deep to find what was hidden inside. I was worth the wait, even if it meant that Jackson would walk away and never return. It was the chance I needed to take.

I picked up my water bottle, took a long drink and then started jogging at a slow pace. Jackson grabbed my hand, intertwining his fingers with mine, and gave it a gentle kiss.

"I'm glad I came along for the run," he said.

"Me too."

"Can I see you again, Jasmine? I mean, after this weekend? Can we have dinner or something?"

"I would like that."

Jackson grabbed my hand a little tighter and we made our way back to the house.

Alyson sat on the front porch with her arms folded across her chest.

"How was the run?"

"Fantastic!" said Jackson. "It was exactly what I needed."

"It was a great run," I cosigned.

She didn't look happy for us. Instead, she affected a businesslike tone. "Jasmine, I'd like to carve out some time to talk about the Grove while I'm here. Lord only knows when I'll be back to the islands for a visit."

"Sure," I said. "Let's talk in the morning over a bowl of boil' fish and grits."

"Sounds good."

I excused myself and went into the house to take a shower. As the hot water cascaded over my naked body, I thought of Jackson. I closed my eyes and let my hands wander to my breasts. His sexy, tender lips had caressed mine in the most intimate way. I silently wished it were his hands caressing me now. Wished I could feel him against me again.

Knowing these thoughts were getting me nowhere but aroused, I hopped out of the shower. I moisturized my body, slipped into a pair of silk pajamas and crept down the hall and into my bedroom. I sat on the side of the bed, and just as I'd begun to check my email and Twitter accounts, I heard a light tap on my door. I opened it just enough to peek through the crack. Seeing Jackson, I opened it all the way.

"I just wanted to say good-night," Jackson whispered.

"Good night." I smiled.

He gently kissed my lips and then headed down the hallway to Edward's room. I watched him walk away, and before he went inside, he turned and looked back at me. When he gave me a wink, I leaned my head against the doorpost.

As the sunlight crept across my nose, I strained to open my eyes. It seemed that morning had sneaked up on me. For a moment I lay in bed, staring at the ceiling. Then I looked at my phone to see what time it was. Nine o'clock. It appeared that I had just enjoyed the first night of uninterrupted sleep in a long time. I attributed it to Jackson.

Was he awake? If so, maybe the two of us could sneak away to one of the local eateries for breakfast. But then I remembered I had a breakfast meeting scheduled with my sister. Still, I wanted to peek in on Jackson.

I hopped out of bed, slipped into my robe and rushed down the hall to the bathroom. I washed my face, brushed my teeth, put a little eyeliner on my eyes and just a dab of lip gloss onto my lips, then crept down the hall toward Edward's room. I peeked my head inside the door, which was ajar. The bed had been freshly made with new linens.

"Looking for someone?" Alyson asked.

"Just seeing if our guest needed anything," I explained.

"Like what?"

"I don't know…towels for bathing, or toiletries."

"Or companionship, maybe?"

I rolled my eyes at my sister.

"He's already gone. Got up at the crack of dawn. Had an emergency," she said.

"Something with the Grove?" I asked.

"Something about his mother," said Alyson. "I'm surprised he didn't mention it. Seems the two of you have gotten pretty cozy. It's not a good idea to fraternize with our contractor, Jasmine."

"Thanks for the advice, Alyson." I headed back toward my room. Alyson followed.

"We all have a vested interest in the Grove, and I'm not going to allow you to mess this up for me."

"For you?"

"Yes, for me. You mess up everything for me."

"Really, Alyson? How so?" I turned to face her.

"I would tell you but I really don't have enough time. I have a plane to catch soon. Which reminds me, I have to cancel our breakfast."

"Tell me why you hate me so much. I'd really like to know."

"Well, for starters, you were born into this family."

"Excuse me."

"I was my daddy's favorite girl before you came along and you took that away." She clenched her teeth. "And you got Jimmy Franklin sent away."

Her bitterness went much deeper than I imagined. Jimmy Franklin was a boy who lived in Bannerman Town, in the southern part of Eleuthera. He was popular and handsome and years ago Alyson was completely in love with him.

"Whatever you told Daddy about him got him sent away, and he had to go live with his grandparents in the US. And I will never forgive you for that. He was the love of my life. We were going to be married after high school."

"Jimmy Franklin deserved to get sent away."

"You are not anyone's judge, Jasmine Talbot," said Alyson. "I know you think you can manipulate men to get what you want in life. But you will not jeopardize the Grove because you can't control yourself."

"And you are not my mother!"

I rushed into my room, slammed the door. I leaned against the door before crumbling to the floor. I hated confrontations, especially with my sister. Too often I allowed her to get away with more than she deserved. I rested my face in my hands. I wanted to go back and tell her exactly what I thought of her—and Jimmy Franklin, too. Wanted to tell her how he had followed me home from middle school that day and forced my panties to the ground and tried to rape me. However, I was much stronger than he ever imagined. A senior in high school, he was much bigger and much older, but he'd underestimated the fact that I had older brothers who'd taught me how to defend myself. After a strong knee to the groin, I pulled myself up from the ground and ran like the wind. I told my daddy everything. The next day, Jimmy Franklin was on a one-way flight to Philadelphia.

Alyson had certainly stirred up memories. Memories that I'd fought very hard to suppress for years were now staring me in the face. All this time I thought I was protecting her. I didn't want her to know the truth. I wanted her to believe that Jimmy loved her, when in fact that couldn't have been further from the truth. He loved me— whatever that meant in his sick, twisted mind. He wanted me so badly that he was willing to violate me. Here I was looking out for her, making sure she never found out what a lowlife he really was, and all the while, she returned the sentiment with bitterness and scorn.

Tears burned the side of my face as I relived that day. I saw Jimmy Franklin's face in my mind, smelled his dreadful scent again.

Her flight wouldn't be leaving soon enough.

Chapter 11

Jackson

"Are you completely out of your mind, Jackson?" My brother Drew was literally yelling into the phone.

"I didn't even know she was sick."

"You would've known had you picked up your phone when Mom called. I completely understand that you're upset and hurt or whatever, but you can't just ignore her like that. What is wrong with you, Jax?"

"You don't understand. You weren't the one lied to."

"How long are you going to make them pay for this?" he asked.

"I'm not making anyone pay. I'm healing."

"Are you coming or what?" asked Drew.

"What time is the surgery?"

"Eight."

"I'll be there."

"Are you sure?" Drew asked.

"I said I'd be there."

I hung up the phone and felt numb. My mother was about to undergo heart surgery and I didn't even know that her heart was damaged. I knew that she'd battled with hypertension over the years, but so had her mother and her mother's mother. It was a generational disease. No one that I knew had heart surgery because of it. But apparently she'd stopped taking her medication on a regular basis and now her arteries were clogged. She'd always been a very responsible person, careful about her diet and her meds. So for her to become so careless about it now was alarming.

I immediately called Tracy. She'd been with me five years—the best assistant I'd ever had. She fit right in with the team and was more like family than an employee. Tracy was a bit older, in her thirties, divorced, with a teenage son, Devante, whom I had mentored. Devante was a good kid, but just had gotten mixed in with the wrong crowd. I had brought him back on track, helped his focus. Now he was looking at colleges.

Tracy kept me on track with my appointments, made my travel arrangements and wasn't afraid to offer her unwarranted opinion about things.

"I'm not trying to get in your business, Jackson, but when was the last time you talked to your mama?"

"I don't know. A long time."

"You gotta do better," said Tracy. "You told me that you used to talk to your mama every single day, and now this. I would be devastated if Devante stopped calling me. He's my world."

Her words pierced my heart. *He's my world.* I had been my mother's world for so long. The baby of the family, I had been the one she bonded with the most.

"I know, Tracy. But I don't really need a lecture right

now. What I need is a flight back to Key West, as soon as
you can get me one."

"Okay, okay. I'm looking now. I'll try to get you a flight
out of there today, but it ain't looking good. Might have to
put you on a red-eye or something."

The flight she found was an afternoon one with a con-
nection in Miami, but it didn't arrive in the Keys until
morning. I lifted my bag from the carousel and placed it
onto my shoulder before I stepped into the warm Florida
sun, breathed in the air of the Keys. I hailed a cab at the
curb and tossed my bag into the trunk. As the driver sped
away from Key West International Airport, my body sank
into the backseat of the car. I rested my head against the
back of the seat and closed my eyes…and Jasmine came
to mind. Jasmine and her phenomenal body. She was nothing like I thought she'd be. Her energy was infectious. She
was insightful.

*Why does the harshest judgment come from people who
love you the most?*

Jasmine's words had stuck with me long after we'd returned from our run that night at her family's home. Made
me look inward; think of my own harsh judgment I'd given
someone I loved. I felt guilty. A multitude of emotions
rushed through me. My thoughts went back to the day in
the hospital, when my ulcers were bleeding and my mother
sat next to my bed and wiped my forehead with a cold, wet
cloth. The pain was so intense, I thought I would die, but
Mom comforted me as best she could.

"You're going to be just fine, baby," she'd said.

"The doctor said I need a blood transfusion, and I don't
want to take my chances with donated blood," I told her.
"I know that you're type A, and I'm type B. Obviously
Pops is type B also. Maybe he can give me some blood."

"I don't know that he can do that."

"Why not?"

She gave me a weak smile and touched my hand with hers. Hers was cold. "Why don't you try and get some rest, honey. We'll talk more later." She stood and was about to leave the room.

"Why can't Pops give me blood? We have the same blood type, right?"

She turned and looked at me. "John's blood type is O, sweetheart."

"That's not possible, Ma. You're mistaken," I told her emphatically.

"John Conner is not your father, honey."

I was confused. John Conner had always been my father. For as long as I could remember he was the only father I knew. He'd raised me. He walked me to school and was there waiting every day to pick me up. He instilled values—taught me how to be a man, gave me the *sex talk* and explained things that I didn't understand. He taught me the value of a hard day's work and a good education. He taught me how to throw a baseball and how to catch it in my mitt. He was the reason I attended Harvard. He was my hero; my mentor. I loved him. I called him Daddy. What was she talking about?

"I don't understand."

"It's a long story, Jax. Let's talk about it another time."

"I have all the time in the world now. I'm just lying here doing nothing. Let's talk about it now." I adjusted my bed, sat straight up, turned the television off.

My mother sighed heavily; her eyes were saddened. She gave me another weak smile.

"I did a horrible thing, Jax." She was nearly in tears. "John and I were very young. Had a family too soon. And your brothers…they were small boys. We experienced some marital problems, and…"

I hung on her every word, not wanting to miss a thing.

"…I stepped out on him."

"You had an affair?" I asked.

"I became pregnant with you while I was with another man."

I stared at my mother, too stunned to move. I couldn't speak for what seemed like an eternity.

"I confessed everything to John and he forgave me. Said that he loved me in spite of everything. We decided that he would raise you as his own. No one would be hurt. No one had to know. Not you. Not your brothers."

"That's why I don't look like him. That's why all three of my brothers look like him and I don't."

John Conner walked into the room, caught the end of my conversation with my mother. When he looked into my eyes, he knew that I knew. His eyes were immediately saddened, but I was sure mine pierced him. My blood began to boil, and I was suddenly filled with anger.

"Son…" John Conner said. I'm sure he wanted to help my mother smooth things over.

"Don't call me that. I'm not your son!" I spat.

"Jackson!" my mother said. "Don't speak to your father that way."

I needed to be away from them. Both of them. I wanted them to leave.

"I need to be alone," I told them. "Please leave."

Tears filled my mother's eyes, and my heart ached for her. I had always been her confidant, her best friend—we talked every single day, sometimes several times. We shared intimate secrets. I told her things that I'd never shared with anyone. And I made it my business to protect her. When she hurt, I hurt. But at that moment, I was drowning in my own pain. I couldn't deal with hers.

"I'm so sorry, Jackson. So many times I wanted to tell you. I just didn't know where to begin."

"You should have begun with the truth," I said and then turned my back to them.

"I've been your father since the day you were born, Jackson," John Conner said. "I loved you then, and I love you now. Nothing has changed."

"What do you mean nothing has changed? This changes everything!" I said.

"It doesn't have to change anything," my mother said.

"Who is he?" I looked at my mother.

"Who is who?"

"My father. My biological father. What's his name?"

She disregarded my question. "He never knew I was pregnant, or that I had given birth to his child."

"So he was deceived, too. You deprived him of a son, just like you deprived me of knowing my father." I had so much bitterness in my heart. "Who is he?"

"Those are old wounds, Jackson. Better left unopened," she explained. "He was married...*is* married, with a family. A prominent man. I wouldn't want you going looking for him."

I didn't have a response. Speechless, I counted the moments until I heard their footsteps leave the room. I fought back tears, convinced myself that men didn't cry. We were made to be strong, to keep it together. But I couldn't keep it together for a second longer. Tears crept down my cheeks, burned like fire against my skin. The pain was no longer in my abdomen, but my heart.

Since then I have relived that day so many times in my head. It was the day I felt as if my life ended and I didn't know how to revive it. It was the day I'd decided to punish my mother, to make her pay for destroying my life. I cut off all communication with her and John Conner. I wanted them to feel the same heartache that I felt. And so far, I'd been successful. No matter how much my mother professed her sorrow, I was relentless. For years, I'd justified my actions with blame. I'd even dropped out of Harvard because it was John Conner's alma mater. I hid behind what I believed. I believed that they should have been forthcoming with me, and because they hadn't, that gave me the right to harbor anger. Just as Jasmine's siblings had judged her, I'd passed judgment on my mother.

The harshest judgment *did* come from those who loved you the most. Though I quickly understood this, I wasn't quite prepared to do anything about it. Instead, it was easier to rid my thoughts of it. I thought about Jasmine Talbot instead. I wasn't ready to face my truths about my mother and John Conner, but I was definitely ready to admit to myself that I had a strong attraction to my friend's younger sister. And not the stuffy older one either. But the one who had driven me crazy since the first day I met her.

After the short drive from the airport, the cab pulled up in front of the Lower Keys Medical Center. As I pulled my bag from the trunk of the car, I spotted my brother Eli puffing on a cigarette.

"Don't you know that smoking is bad for your health? Causes cancer."

"Yeah, that's what they tell me." He grinned and wrapped his arm tightly around my neck and kissed my cheek. "Missed you, little brother."

Of all my brothers, Eli was the most easygoing. He stood at five eleven and a half, with dark skin like John Conner's and a muscular build. He was athletic and very careful about his diet, but smoked cigarettes during stressful situations.

"I missed you, too," I told him. "When did you get in?"

"This morning. Caught a red-eye out of JFK."

"Mya and the baby come, too?" I asked.

"Nah, she's taking some theater class at Columbia right now. Couldn't get away."

"And little Eli? He's going to be graduating college before I see him again."

"You'll have to make a trip upstate soon. We have an extra room. You can stay as long as you like."

"I'll think about it."

I avoided asking about my mother. I wanted to block her condition and pending surgery from my mind for as long as I could.

"Little Eli is growing like a weed, man." He flicked the butt of his cigarette onto the pavement. "Eighteen months and already formulating phrases. Man, you should hear him trying to talk. Mya's really good with him, too."

The two of us walked inside the hospital.

"I'm happy for you. You found the woman of your dreams," I told Eli.

"I did, indeed." He smiled. "What about you, Jax? When will you find the woman of your dreams?"

"I don't know that I ever will. Life's too busy. The days are endless."

"Life's too short not to find a woman to share life with," said Eli. "Not one single prospect?"

"Not really looking."

"Well, maybe you *should* look."

For some strange reason, Jasmine's face popped into my head. Her gorgeous smile became visible to me at that moment, but I brushed it from my mind. She wasn't my type—we were as different as different could be.

The huge, silver elevator doors opened and we stepped on. A doctor was being paged over the loudspeaker.

"Drew didn't tell me much on the phone. Just said she

was having this heart procedure and I needed to get down here as soon as possible," I explained. "How's she doing?"

"They've prepped her," said Eli calmly, "gave her something to put her to sleep."

"You know, I haven't seen her or John much since…"

"Since you found out he wasn't your biological father? Yeah, I know. It's all Ma talks about when I call her—how much she regrets not telling you sooner."

"It changed everything for me. Made me question everything in my life. I don't know who I am."

"You're a Conner, that's who you are! So what, Daddy's not your biological father. Hasn't he given you everything that a father should give a son?"

"You don't understand."

"I understand that you and I had the same upbringing. We were afforded the same opportunities, and we were instilled with the same values. What am I missing?"

"You're missing everything."

"Yeah, they should've told you the truth. No doubt. I'd be pissed if it were me, too."

"But it's not you. So let's just drop it."

It was a conversation that was never comfortable. I felt as if my entire life had been a lie, and it caused me to be uncertain about my identity. I didn't know who I was or where I came from—and at times I wondered where I was headed. I only knew the life that John and Sarah Conner had constructed for me. And that life had been built on a lie.

But right now I had to look ahead. And that meant seeing my mother.

My mother lay there, motionless, her eyes closed, her breathing heavy and an oxygen tube in her nose. She looked more helpless than I'd anticipated, and guilt immediately overtook me. I had ignored her calls when she needed me most. She was about to face one of the most daunting events in her life, and I hadn't been there for her. She'd struggled with heart disease for some time. She and I had talked at length over the years about her making some healthy lifestyle changes to get her hypertension under control. But she was stubborn, just like me. Thought that she could control things on her own. She'd passed that trait on to me, too.

I kissed her forehead, and she opened her eyes.

"Jax," she whispered. She didn't smile, but I knew that her heart was filled with joy that I was there.

"Don't talk," I told her. "Just rest. I'll be here after the surgery is over. We can talk then."

I needed some air, so I stepped out of the room and strolled down to the family waiting room where my brothers were. Eli chatted with his wife on his cell phone. I gave my brother Sean a strong embrace and glanced over at Drew, who paced the floor while talking on the phone.

"Good to see you, Jax," said Sean. "Ma's been asking about you. I'm glad you made it so she doesn't have a hissy fit."

"I had to be here."

"The surgery should go well. She's floating on some good drugs right now." Sean was the prankster in the family. He took his cell phone out and showed me a picture. "I took a picture of her with her hair all over her head. I can't wait to show it to her."

"You are still stupid," I told him.

"I've got to keep the old woman on her toes."

"Jackson Conner." Drew finished his phone conversation and then pulled me into an embrace. "Good to see you, bro. How's business?"

"Business is good. I'm right in the middle of a new project," I explained.

"Oh, that's right—that Bahamas thing you were telling me about."

"Yes. Doing some work for an old friend."

Drew was an unyielding playboy, vowing never to settle down with one woman. He preferred the challenge of playing the field.

"I hear there are some beautiful women over there in the Bahamas. Is that true?" he asked.

"I've really been too busy to notice."

"What?" asked Drew. "Nobody is that busy."

"You know Jax is a workaholic." Eli walked over after finishing his call and patted me on the back. "He's always been very focused. Regimented. You could learn a thing or two from your younger brother, Drew."

"All work and no play makes for a very dull life." Drew plopped down in a chair and started flipping through his phone. "He could learn a thing or two from me."

I walked over toward the window, deciding now was the time to check in with Lance and see how things were going at the Grove.

"Everything's under control here," Lance told me. "How's your mom?"

"She's about to go in for surgery."

"You should focus on being there for her. Don't worry about things here. We're good."

Lance was a good construction manager. Because his work ethic was very much like mine, I had no reservations about leaving the job site for a couple of days. We talked for a few minutes longer and then I ended my call. My back was to the room, and when I turned around, my eyes met John Conner's. He walked toward me, held his hand out to me. I took his hand in mine and gave him a strong handshake.

"Good to see you, Jackson. I'm glad you could make it. Means the world to your mother…and me."

I just nodded. There was so much I wanted to say but didn't. It wasn't the time or place.

He walked away and headed back to my mother's room, where he stayed till she was taken into the operating room.

The surgery was a success, and many hours later my mother recovered in the intensive care unit. A breathing tube in her mouth and several wires attached to her body, she lay there peacefully sleeping. I was able to visit briefly, but needed to share the time with my brothers. We were told that the breathing tube would be removed within twenty-four hours, and until then she wouldn't be able to talk.

My heart ached. It was hard to see my mother so help-less. I wished I could turn back the hands of time. I wouldn't have been so rigid or allowed my anger to get the best of me. I wouldn't have let so much time go by without talk-ing to her, without telling her that I loved her in spite of everything. And as soon as she opened her eyes, I vowed I would tell her so.

I woke, curled up in a chair in the corner of the room. When I opened my eyes my mother was looking at me.

She smiled. "You looked so peaceful, I didn't want to wake you."

"Ma." I sat up straight in my chair, feeling a crick in my neck.

"Where is everybody?"

"They went home to grab a bite to eat and catch some shut-eye. I wanted to be here when you opened your eyes," I said. "How you feeling?"

"A lot of pressure in my chest area. Feels like it's burning."

"Should I get the nurse?"

"No, they told me it would feel like this for a while until I begin to recover." She looked me over. "You're looking a little thin. You been eating?"

"Not as much as I should. I miss your cooking." I laughed at my comment and tried to avoid the elephant in the room, but it was useless. "Mom, I'm sorry for treating you the way I have since…since everything went on. I've been selfish and judgmental."

"I'm sorry for hiding the truth from you. I just wanted you to have a normal life without having to concern yourself with identity issues." She winced at the pain. "I was wrong. I shouldn't have kept it from you. You deserved to know."

"I understand why you did it. I know you were protecting me."

"But I ended up hurting you more in the end. And now I've destroyed your relationship with John, who loves you more than you'll ever know."

"I know he does," I said. "It must've taken a lot of humility to raise another man's child like that."

"After he decided to do it, he never gave it a second thought." She winced again. The pain must've been tremendous and my heart went out to her. "But you know what… As much as John Conner loves you, he's not your father. And you have a right to know who your father is. His name is Patrick H. Wells. The *H* stands for Harvey."

"My middle name," I said.

Mom didn't respond. Instead she continued. "He's the mayor of some small town in Louisiana. I don't know how to reach him, but he shouldn't be hard to find. I'm sure you can just look him up on that internet."

"Patrick Harvey Wells, huh?" My heart smiled.

"Yes."

"Does he know anything about me?"

"He doesn't even know you exist, baby. So you shouldn't have too many expectations," she said. "He's married, he has a family, and he's a political figure. And that makes things very complicated."

"He deserves to know that he has a son out there in the world."

"Be sure to guard your heart, Jackson."

It was the last thing she said before she began to doze off.

Chapter 12

Jasmine

With walls painted in lovely, warm hues, my office was beautiful. The hardwoods shone as bright as the Bahamian sunshine that crept through the windows on the back of the house. The dark walnut desk was a perfect counterbalance to the floors. And the art I'd hung on the walls—the lovely, contemporary pieces that I'd picked up at last year's Los Angeles Arts Festival—were just the right touches to bring the room together. I leaned back in my brown leather chair and closed my eyes. Thoughts of Jackson raced through my mind, as I got lost in my work. Over the few months since the reconstruction of the first house started, I had literally become a workaholic. I'd already developed a solid marketing plan for the property and had begun keeping long hours. I already loved working at the Grove. It felt like home.

The end to another week, and although Jackson had been gone for only a few days, it seemed like months. I'd so hoped that he'd call or text, but I hadn't heard a word from him. I missed seeing his face at the Grove and wondered how long it would be before he returned.

The Clydesdale was close to completion. The floors in the entire house had been refinished, the walls were painted, fixtures in place, the wiring and plumbing redone. I had already begun working with an interior decorator that had given me her vision for the place. The Symonette Room had been a tribute to the Caribbean goombay artist George Symonette and designed in rich colors and musical art. Other rooms would pay tribute to legendary goombay and Rake and Scrape artists of the Caribbean. I was passionate about designing that house, particularly since I had a love for music.

Jorge walked past my office. "It's late, Miss Talbot, and I hate to leave you here. There's a storm approaching. It's already coming down pretty hard. Can I get you a taxi to the ferry?"

"Thanks, Jorge, but I'll be fine. I'm going to stay the night. No need fighting the storm tonight." I smiled.

"Are you sure?"

"Positive," I assured him. "Go on home."

"Okay." But he was reluctant to leave and lingered in the doorway.

"I'll be fine, seriously. Go on," I told him.

"I'll see you in the morning?" he asked.

"Bright and early."

"Have a fantastic evening, *mi querida*."

"You too, Jorge."

I followed him to the front door and locked it behind him. I turned on the porch light and started back toward the stairs when I heard the sound of someone tampering with the lock. I swung open the door and was surprised to see Jackson standing beneath the bright porch light. A taxicab slowly eased away from the curb.

"What are you doing here?" I asked.

"I came by to check things out, see what kind of progress the men made while I was gone," he said, stepping inside. He began to look around, moving into each room. "They did an amazing job of finishing things up here."

"Yes, they did," I agreed.

"We're going to begin work on the Talbot House first thing Monday morning. They should've already started pulling up the linoleum in the kitchen and bathrooms over there."

I was barely listening to Jackson. His mouth was moving but I was too busy staring at his facial features. The way his eyes danced when he talked about the Grove. He had just as much passion about the place as the Talbot children did about their inheritance. His lips looked kissable, and his cologne lingered in every room. I realized just how much I'd missed him.

"Why are you still here?" he asked. "Didn't you hear the weather forecast?"

A harsh storm threatened to sweep across the island. Long before Jorge said good-night, I had already decided to stay at the Grove instead of rushing to catch the water ferry. It was safer. I had grown up in the Caribbean, so I knew how abrasive the weather could be during a storm. I had been through many a hurricane season and my share of tropical storms. I had already called Daddy hours before and told him not to worry about meeting me at the ferry.

"I'm just going to stay over. No need heading home in this," I told Jackson.

As if to underscore my words, thunder roared and a flash of lightning shot through the front window.

"Yeah, that's probably a good idea," he said. "Do you mind if I bunk here for the night, too? It's getting pretty violent out there."

"I don't mind at all. The beds that I ordered came earlier this week, so there's a king bed in the Symonette Room on the third floor. You can sleep there," I told him. "You hungry?"

"Famished."

"I'll cook you something."

"Really? You don't have to go to the trouble."

"You have a better idea? The weather's too bad to go out and get anything. I have some grouper in the kitchen, and the ingredients for conch salad. What do you say?"

"I say, thank you." He smiled. "And I'll help. Maybe you can teach me a thing or two."

"Maybe I can." I walked into the kitchen and Jackson followed. I tossed him a black apron and then tied a red one around my waist. "Let's get started."

Jackson thoroughly washed the fish while I prepared the ingredients for the conch salad. I showed him how to fillet and season the grouper with rich Bahamian spices. He was an attentive student, taking in every detail.

"Go ahead and place it in the oven," I told him. "I know you're hungry right now, so I have some papaya in the fridge that you can nibble on until dinnertime. I'll be in the Grand Room for a bit."

The Grand Room was the home to my grandfather's baby grand piano. It was the room where I envisioned entertainment would take place—artists from all over the world would give live performances. There would be round tables covered in crisp white tablecloths and a huge dance floor. I loved the Grand Room just as much as I loved playing the piano. My brother Nate and I played the piano. We were the only two of the Talbot children who had taken after our grandfather. I wasn't a professional, but could play the piano enough to get by.

Taking a seat at the grand piano, I began to play a familiar song—softly mouthing the words of John Legend's "So High." Suddenly during the chorus, I heard a voice rise above mine, with falsetto vocals that captured John Legend's notes perfectly. It was one of the most beautiful voices I'd ever heard.

I glanced over at Jackson, who was standing in the doorway, singing his heart out. I continued to play as he sang effortlessly. After the song finished, I heard clapping.

"Bravo!" he said.

"No, bravo to you!" I was astounded. "What was that?"

"Oh, that was nothing."

"You're in the wrong line of work. You need to be on somebody's record label."

"It's a hobby." He walked over and took a seat next to me at the piano. "What else can you play?"

I started playing the notes of another Legend tune, "Ordinary People."

"You like this guy, huh?"

"He's easy to learn," I explained. "I play by ear."

"You're good."

"I'm okay."

As the storm swept across the ocean, we spent the entire night in the Grand Room. I played the notes while Jackson sang the vocals of every song in my repertoire. After I hit the last key of the last song, I rested for a moment. We chatted about our lives and surprisingly Jackson opened up to me.

"The day she told me that John Conner wasn't my father, I thought my world had come to an end. It's hard to explain." He told me about the lie that had destroyed his relationship with his mother.

"I would feel the same way if I found out that the man I called Daddy wasn't my biological father. I'd be devastated," I told him. "My dad is my best friend."

"Same with my mother. I felt betrayed. And I wasn't very nice to her." Jackson held his head low. "I'm ashamed of the way I treated her…not taking her calls. I didn't even know she was having heart surgery until the last minute."

"At least you were able to make it there…to be by her side. I bet it meant the world to her."

"It meant everything to her."

"Are you still angry with your stepfather?"

"Not so much," he said. "I'm just really curious about my real father. I need to have a conversation with him. I keep imagining what he must be like…how he talks, looks. If I have any of his traits."

"Have you looked him up on Google?"

"Not yet."

"Why not?"

"I don't know. Fear, I guess."

"Don't you want to know?" I asked. I grabbed his hands in mine for a moment.

"Maybe."

"I'll be right back." I rushed upstairs to my office and grabbed my laptop, brought it back downstairs. "What's his name?"

"Patrick H. Wells," he said.

I logged on to my computer and opened my Safari browser. Typed *Patrick H. Wells* into the search bar. I sorted through the results of the images until I found a photo of the man. He was an older version of Jackson—same skin tone, eyes and smile, same curly hair. The similarities were astounding.

"You want to see?"

He looked at me and his eyes reminded me of a small

boy's eyes. When he nodded, I turned my computer around and he stared into his father's eyes on the screen.

"Wow," he murmured. "I look like him."

"Yes, you do. You should reach out to him."

"You think so?"

"Yes. It's the only way you'll feel some peace about this. Maybe it will answer some of your questions."

"Maybe," he agreed. "I should do it in person. Not over the phone."

"I agree." I closed my computer and placed it on top of the baby grand. I moved closer to Jackson. I hugged him tightly, hoping that I could ease his fears a bit. He felt good in my arms.

My eyes met his and his lips gently touched mine. The kiss was sweeter than I remembered from the beach almost a week before. I knew it well because I'd replayed it in my mind a million times since then. I'd savored every single memory of our first kiss.

Unexpectedly, his fingertips began to glide gently across my breasts, causing my nipples to stiffen from his touch. With hesitation, he waited for my response. I closed my eyes and eased closer to him. He accepted the unspoken invitation and effortlessly lifted my shirt over my head, then loosened my bra. The coolness of the room caused me to shiver; goose bumps danced up and down my arms. His lips abandoned my mouth and began to explore the roundness of my breasts, taking the nipples in between his teeth at intervals. His fingers gently caressed my midsection, toyed with my navel and then rigorously loosened the button of my khaki shorts. After removing my shorts, Jackson boldly explored the soft area beneath my delicate, sheer panties. I felt guilty for not returning the pleasure right away, but I selfishly wanted to enjoy every moment.

The sensation of his fingertips inside of me only caused me to moan and kiss him deeper.

Finally my hands explored the strength of his chest and arms that I'd admired on too many occasions since meeting Jackson Conner. I loosened the belt of his jeans and reached inside for him, carefully freeing him, holding him and stroking just enough to make him shudder.

"What are you doing to me?" he whispered. His lips were wet against my earlobe.

I had no words. I hoped that the fire in my eyes was answer enough. It must've been because he quickly produced a condom and put it on. In one motion he lifted my body and placed me onto his lap. He entered me and we both sighed as our bodies moved together in a sexy motion. His lips explored my ample breasts again—one by one—nibbling each one as if enjoying his favorite indulgence. He gently began to caress the small of my back and then explored the roundness of my soft behind. We made sweet love as the thunder roared just outside the window of the Clydesdale.

The sun gently crept its way across my nose and I opened my eyes. The sun was now beaming as if thunder hadn't roared all night. Wearing nothing more than the diamond earrings my brother Nate had given me for my birthday, I struggled to figure out where I was. The sheets that covered my naked body smelled of fabric softener.

"Good morning, Sunshine." Jackson appeared in the doorway of the Symonette Room, wearing an apron with nothing underneath. He carried food on a tray.

"What time is it?" I asked, searching for my phone.

"Eight or so," he said. "I made breakfast."

"You can cook?"

"I make a mean omelet. It's my pride and joy."

"Really?"

He caused me to blush for no apparent reason at all. It could have been because I was completely naked underneath the sheet that just barely covered me. And quite possibly because the red apron barely covered his nakedness. He was undeniably sexy. His strong arms protruded from beneath the apron, as did his muscular legs. Arms that had held me and legs that had wrapped around me as I experienced pleasure like never before. I had only recently run my fingers through those curly locks of his and gazed into those light brown eyes until well into the night. Those lips had been tender against mine, and those fingertips had danced in places that had never been touched like that before.

"It looks wonderful."

I was greeted with a perfect omelet accompanied by fresh fruit and a slice of wheat toast. "A glass of freshly squeezed orange juice for you," he said with a smile.

"You squeezed oranges?"

"I said it was freshly squeezed. I didn't say I did it." He laughed. "Said it on the carton."

"Okay." I laughed, too.

The hard exterior that Jackson once had was slowly being chipped away, and I was completely drawn to the man underneath. He was interesting and funny—a perfect gentleman. And, as I'd discovered last night, an impeccable lover. One who was gracious, yet unyielding. He wasn't lazy or selfish. The traits I'd seen in his work at the Grove were the same ones he'd displayed in the bedroom.

"I thought about it all night, and I've decided I'm going to Louisiana next weekend. I'm going to pay my father a visit," said Jackson.

"That's fantastic, Jackson. You should."

"Will you go with me?"

"Really? You want me to go?"

"You were so sweet and so supportive last night," he said, "I wouldn't want to do this without you."

"Yes, I will go with you."

"Thank you." He grabbed my chin and kissed the tip of my nose. "I'm hitting the shower. We have a busy day ahead of us."

"We do?"

"Yes. You're taking me on a tour of the island. I want to know everything about this place that you call home. And about you." He grinned. "And don't leave out any details. I want to know about the old boyfriends, too."

I laughed and watched as Jackson's tight rear end exited the room.

Chapter 13

Jackson

I sat on the passenger's side of our rented vehicle as Jasmine breezed through the streets of Gregory Town, James Cistern and then Governor's Harbour. She gave me the guided tour of the island, pointing out the significance of every pastel-colored structure along the way. The Haynes Library, a pink-and-white building adorned with turquoise hurricane shutters, I discovered, was one of the island's historical landmarks. It was originally built in 1897 and refurbished in the nineties.

"They have an internet café in there if you ever need to plug in your laptop," said my beautiful tour guide. "It's a great place to relax and chill. I avoided it like the plague when I was younger. Anything to do with reading, I wasn't interested in."

"I would think a girl like you would love to read."

"No, you have me mistaken with my older sister, Alyson, or my younger sister, Whitney, who teaches little kids in Texas. I'm more interested in a great party than a great book."

"Did you want to go to college, or did you want to do something different like your brother Denny?"

"I wanted to get away from home! Far away!"

"Why did you choose Spelman?"

"I chose Spelman because my brother Nate chose Morehouse and the two schools were close. I wanted to be near him. Nate and I are very close—only eighteen months apart. And I heard about the Greek step shows at Morehouse and how popular their homecoming was. And I heard that the parties were off the charts."

"Okay, so you weren't interested in a quality education at all," I teased.

"I didn't go there looking for a quality education, but I got one anyway." She laughed.

"Thank goodness! It's why we aren't allowed to make our own choices when we're young and dumb."

"My first year of college was nearly impossible. I just barely passed my classes. I underestimated college. Thought if I made the right connections, I could breeze through it. It was that way all my life. My father always had a friend around the corner or someone who would look out for me. Every one of my teachers here on the island was good friends with my dad, so school was a breeze," she explained, "but I got a taste of real life very quickly. I almost dropped out."

"I was in my last year of law school when I dropped out of Harvard."

"Are you serious?"

"Very."

Harvard was a hard subject to discuss. In fact, I'd never

had the courage to bring it up to anyone before. I hid behind it for so many years, ashamed. But Jasmine was as easy as a summer's breeze to talk to. She made me feel that I could say anything, and she never judged me.

I told her everything, and she listened.

"I held on to that anger for years, only recently letting go," I told her. "It was something you said the other day that made me think about things differently."

"Something I said?"

"Yeah. You said that sometimes the harshest judgment comes from those who love you the most. It made me really stop and think about things. I was handing out my own dose of harsh judgment to my mother. She didn't deserve it. And when I saw her lying in that hospital bed, struggling to open her eyes after surgery, I felt like a total and complete jerk."

"The important thing is that you realized it, and you made your peace."

Either Jasmine was as philosophical as hell, or I was falling for her. Hard. I stared at her as she maneuvered through town. Her hair blew gently in the wind. She wore a sheer cover-up with a bikini underneath. She had to be the sexiest woman I'd seen in a long time—with a shapely body, toned arms and legs, solid abs and a set of perfectly sized breasts.

"Where to next, Madam Tour Guide?"

"A quick tour of my old neighborhood in Governor's Harbour and then to Gregory Town. My cousin owns a surf shop there. We're going to rent a board and go for a spin."

"Excuse me? A spin where?"

"On the ocean, silly. We're going surfing. Haven't you ever done that before?"

"Not…never…"

"Well, there's a first time for everything," she said matter-of-factly.

"You don't understand. I don't know how to surf. And it's really not my thing."

"Where's your audacity?" she asked. "If you're going to hang out with Jasmine Talbot, you have to let go of those inhibitions."

"Inhibitions? Me?"

"I've been told that you're a workaholic, among other things."

"I see. So you've been inquiring about me." I smiled a little at the thought.

"Not really."

"Yes, really. It's the only way you would know that I'm a workaholic...*among other things*."

"People talk. They offer unwarranted information sometimes."

"Is that right?"

"That's right."

"I want to kiss you so bad right now."

She gave me a smile and continued to drive toward Governor's Harbour. She pointed out every landmark and showed me where every one of her childhood friends grew up. She drove past her old elementary school and high school. I saw the park where she had her first kiss. Finally, she pulled up in front of an old yellow house with white trim. It desperately needed a paint job and the porch looked as if it might fall apart if the wind blew too hard.

"Who lives here?" I asked.

"It's Darren Spencer's old home. He was my high school sweetheart," she said nonchalantly. "His cousins still live there. His father invested well in the hotel industry and moved his family to Miami several years ago. They have a huge presence in the hospitality industry, and they own a stream of hotels and restaurants all over the state of Florida and a few hotels in the Bahamas. Though they've accumulated all this wealth, they're very modest people and they love the Bahamas."

"I see." I was so jealous at that moment. I'd thought I wanted to know about every one of her former boyfriends, but the truth was I didn't want to know about any of them. The thought of them touching her and doing the same things to her body that I'd just done unnerved me.

"Darren attended college in the States, too. Studied economics. Now he manages a few of their hotels in Florida and the one in Nassau."

"I see." They were the only words I could think of to say. The more details she shared about Darren, the less I wanted to hear about him.

"We were supposed to both return here after college... get married, have babies. Blah, blah, blah," she said. "Instead he broke my heart. So end of story."

"I see." I said it again. I had no other words.

"His parents never cared for me. They didn't think I was good enough for their son. Called me promiscuous. But they couldn't have been more wrong about me. I was completely devoted to their son. He was my first, and my last until after I graduated from Spelman. Sure, I liked to party, but promiscuous I was not. It was Darren who decided to sow his oats with every girl on his college campus."

"Hmm."

"So he went away and married a girl from the US. And now they're divorcing."

I was relieved when she pulled away from the house. It took a few moments for me to regain my composure. I finally did as we drove down Queen's Highway and eventually approached Surfer's Beach.

Jasmine's cousin Steven helped me to choose the right board for a novice, and with nerves twisting my gut I followed Jasmine down to the shore. Confident and carefree, she went out to show me how it was done. She lay flat on her board, her stomach pressing against it while her arms paddled through the water. After a few moments of waiting for the perfect wave, she lifted her body up onto her knees and soon she was standing on the board and floating across the ocean. She looked like a pro. After warming up on a few more waves, she made her way back to shore to help me get started.

I followed her lead and lay with my stomach flat on the board. I imitated Jasmine and paddled through the water with my arms. As soon as a wave rushed toward me, I lifted my body up and onto my knees. However, my attempt to stand up on the board failed, and I tumbled into the water with a huge splash. Jasmine laughed as I tried to regain my composure.

"Take your time," she said.

Slowly I pressed my stomach against the board again, lifted up onto my knees, and this time I was able to stand up on the board. My legs shook and it took all I had just to maintain balance, but I stood. I wasn't a pro, but I'd conquered the board.

Afterward, we relaxed on beach towels—our backs against the warm, pink sand, our eyes staring into the blueness of the sky. We discussed our goals and shared our dreams with each other. I casually reached over and grabbed her hand, interlocked my fingers with hers. I could've remained that way forever. It felt good being with her, and the mood was perfect. It felt as if our hearts had connected.

As the sun began to set, we returned our rental car and headed back to Harbour Island by ferry. Exhausted from our full day, we stopped at one of the local eateries for a quick bite to eat. A burger seemed more appealing than the native fare this time. Not that I didn't enjoy a nice Bahamian meal. In fact, I'd become quite accustomed to it.

However, at the moment I was in need of something that felt more like home. Jasmine, who was more health conscious than anyone I knew, and who avoided beef, ordered a bowl of fish stew. We both enjoyed a glass of wine.

"I had fun today," I told her as I took a bite of my burger.

"Me too." She leaned back in her chair, took a sip of her wine. "Thank you for letting me show you my home."

"I feel like I've known you all my life," I told her. "You're so easy to be with."

"I feel the same about you."

"I must confess, I didn't feel that way about you in the beginning." I laughed. "I actually placed a call to Edward and told him he should have a word with you. I told him you were cramping my style."

"Really? The nerve of you!" She laughed heartily. "I almost made that same call."

"You should be ashamed of yourself the way you came in trying to run things." I began to mock her. "The wood paneling stays... I want the rooms painted in bright colors... I need that old desk moved upstairs right this minute... I need an office that overlooks the ocean... I'm the princess...blah, blah, blah."

"I never said I was a princess!" she said.

"You didn't have to. You behaved like one."

She grabbed a French fry from my plate and tossed it at me. We laughed and talked the evening away. I wanted to spend the night with her again, but wasn't quite sure of her intentions, so I avoided the subject. As the night drew near, we both knew that we couldn't necessarily spend the evening at Ma Ruby's burger joint. So we needed to figure something out.

"Are you headed back to Governor's Harbour tonight?" I asked.

"No, I packed a weekend bag. I'll be staying at the Grove

another night," she said. Heaviness filled her eyes. "And you?"

"I would like to spend the night at the Grove, too." There. I'd put it out there into the universe. "How would you feel about that?"

"I would like that very much."

Her words eased the tension. My heart smiled.

When we reached the Grove, we both dropped our shoes at the door, the hardwoods cold against my bare feet. She headed up the stairs and I grabbed her from behind. As I wrapped my arms tightly around her waist, I planted little kisses onto the back of her neck. I was immediately aroused. She turned to face me and my lips found hers. I sank my tongue deep inside her mouth and released her only long enough to pull her cover-up over her head. Then I was kissing her again. When I loosened her bikini top from around her neck, I nibbled on nipples that quickly became firm from my touch. I dipped my hand underneath the elastic of her bikini bottom and explored the goodness between her thighs. She squirmed from the tenderness of my touch, fueling my fire all the more. She moved up two steps, her bottom falling onto the wood of the staircase. I steadied myself above her and removed her bikini bottoms, then planted my fingers inside her warmth again as my lips consumed hers.

I planted a stream of kisses from her chin to her neck. My lips briefly kissed each of her breasts and my tongue lingered around her navel. I kissed the insides of her thighs and she lightly moaned. I stretched her legs apart and planted my tongue in the place where my fingers had explored just moments before. Jasmine closed her eyes tightly and leaned her head back onto the staircase. Soon, her whole body shuddered as she reached the highest of peaks. She must've known how badly I wanted to be inside of her because she began to caress my hardness—gently at first, and then vigorously. She pulled my briefs down and my manhood stood strong in front of her face. She kissed me there, gently took me into her mouth. I held on to the railing and steadied myself, trying not to lose control. When I couldn't take it anymore, I grabbed her petite frame in my arms. Her brown legs wrapped themselves around my waist. I carried her the rest of the way up the stairs and gently placed her onto the bed in the Symonette Room. I lifted her arms above her head and held them there, restraining her. I entered her with vigor. Made sweet love to a woman who'd managed to swiftly hijack my heart overnight.

Chapter 14

Jasmine

I eased out of bed and began to retrieve my clothing from the floor. I quietly searched my overnight bag for clean underwear, careful not to wake Jackson. Then I tiptoed toward the bedroom door.

"Going somewhere?"

I turned toward him. "Sorry, I was trying not to wake you," I said. "I have to go."

"Go where?"

"Church. The Talbots attend church every Sunday morning. And if you're a Talbot and you're anywhere on this island, you're expected to be there."

"Okay," he said. "When will I see you again?"

"Soon." I smiled at him. It warmed my heart that he was anxious to see me again and I hadn't even left yet. "We're having this farewell dinner today for Denny. He leaves for the Royal Bahamas first thing in the morning. Edward and Alyson are both flying in."

"I'll miss you."

"Come with me."

"To church? After the nasty little things we did last night, I don't think so." He laughed. "Besides, are you ready to flaunt me around in front of your family? I don't know how my buddy Edward would take seeing me with his little sister."

"I wouldn't care. It's my life."

"It's why they don't respect your choices," he said. "I wouldn't want them to think this is some fly-by-night sort of fling. That's not what this is, is it?"

He was right. I had not had a moment to analyze *this* and what it might be, but knew that it definitely wasn't a fly-by-night anything. I was beginning to feel things for Jackson that weren't like anything I'd felt with anyone before. I didn't need him to pay my rent or get me the next gig. I needed only his presence, his touch and his beautiful smile. I needed him to hold me the way he had and to interlock his fingers with mine. I felt protected when I was with him. I enjoyed his conversation and longed for his lips to touch mine. I needed him in ways that I'd never needed any man.

"That is definitely not what this is." I cleared my throat; it had gotten choked up at the thought of our lovemaking.

"I'll be here when you return."

Jackson lay in the bed, propped up on his elbow, the sheerness of the sheet just barely covering his waist. Then he rested his arms casually behind his head, as if posing for a photo shoot. I took a mental picture—one that I would sneak a peek at throughout the day. I gave him a gentle smile and then headed for the shower.

As the warm water drizzled over my body, I thought of

Jackson. With my arms wrapped around my own waist, I smiled. I contemplated Jackson's words. Thought about what it was we were doing. Sexually he sent me to new heights, but more than that, I enjoyed our conversations. I longed for his smile, and his laughter was infectious. I experienced a new awareness. To call it love would be premature, but it was definitely a strong *something*.

I slid into the pew next to my father. His eyes lit up when he saw me, and he planted a gentle kiss on my forehead. My mother looked around him to give me a look of displeasure. I was late. I knew I would be when I stood in the shower too long, contemplating my feelings for the man who lay naked in the next room. My mother frowned, but she'd have been more devastated had she known where I was all night. I smiled wickedly at the thought. I gave a little wave to Alyson, who sat on the other side of my mother. She gave me a fake smile, but I pretended it was real. I often pretended that she didn't hate me so much, and that we were close. I envied my friends and their sisters who chatted daily, did brunch and shopped together, and bounced ideas off each other. I wished I had that with either of my sisters. Alyson was much too rigid, and Whitney and I were nothing alike. She was conservative; never pushed the envelope. I was the opposite.

Strong arms hugged my shoulders from behind and someone kissed my cheek. It was my brother Edward, who was dressed in a tailored gray suit and smelled of expensive cologne. I turned around and glanced at his face, which wasn't so clean-shaven anymore—he was growing a beard, which made him look distinguished and handsome. I blew Edward a kiss. Denny, who sat next to Edward, gave my shoulder a tight squeeze.

"Where you been?" Denny tried whispering but it was all but a whisper.

I placed my finger over my lips and mouthed, "Shhh."

"You went surfing yesterday," my father whispered in my ear. It wasn't a question.

"How'd you know?"

"Small island," he said.

If he knew that I went surfing, then he knew I hadn't gone alone. Keeping Jackson a secret would be virtually impossible in a place like Eleuthera.

Good thing no one knew what had transpired last night at the Grove.

The windows were open to give the illusion of a small breeze. The ceiling fans seemed to work extra hard just to cool things off, but I used my program to fan myself anyway. Although I'd chosen a short-sleeved blouse and a knee-length skirt, the warmth inside the church was brutal. A boisterous medley of the pipe organ, drums and tambourines filled that small space. People patted their feet against the old hardwoods and caused a loud eruption. The choir sang with intensity, and at least two sisters caught the Holy Ghost in our little Baptist church in Governor's Harbour. It was the church I'd attended my whole life, where I'd been baptized and took my first Communion. First Baptist Church had been home for many generations of Talbots. And Pastor Johnson had been like family—a brother to my father. He wiped sweat from his brow with an old handkerchief as he preached an intense sermon.

Services never lasted very long on Sunday mornings. Pastor Johnson respected our time and allowed us to spend the better part of the day with our families.

At the Talbot home, my father and Edward retired in front of the television set and watched the soccer game and sipped on Bahamian beers, while my mother, Alyson and I started dinner in the kitchen. Gospel music belted from an old radio that rested in the windowsill above the kitchen sink.

"Jasmine, I need you to start the macaroni and cheese," said my mother.

I immediately tied an apron around my waist and washed my hands. I began to dice onions, sweet peppers and celery. Alyson seasoned the chicken with Caribbean spices while my mother stirred the huge pot of collard greens that she'd started long before church.

"Just about there," she said as she secured the lid. "Church was wonderful this morning, don't you think, girls?"

"It's just so traditional," Alyson complained. "Not like my mega church in Miami. We have huge screens where you can see our pastor and hear his message clearly."

"I heard Pastor Johnson's message pretty clearly this morning," I said.

Alyson rolled her eyes at me and then turned to my mother. "And it was just so hot in there! Why haven't they installed central air-conditioning in that place?"

"We have central air, but we're conserving energy."

"Are you serious, Ma?" Alyson asked.

"Yes. That's why we have ceiling fans."

"Those ceiling fans are a joke," said Alyson as she flipped the chicken over and seasoned the other side. "They don't work."

I couldn't agree more, but I'd never give Alyson the benefit of knowing that.

"Mother, when you come to Miami, I'm going to take you to my church. We have roughly five thousand members, and I serve as head of the ushers, which is two hundred members strong."

"Two hundred members on the usher board?" my mother asked.

"We need more," Alyson added. "The ones we have are overworked."

"I don't think it takes all that," I said. "I love our little Baptist church here on the island. It's our family church, and traditional. Our grandfather's grandfather attended there. I think you miss a lot in the big churches."

"What do you mean it doesn't take all that?" she asked.

"I mean I love the simplicity of our church."

"Of course you do," she said. "But life isn't simple."

"Five thousand members sounds like corporate America, not church," I added.

"Church *is* a business and should be run as such. Not like First Baptist is run. Daddy shouldn't have to run over to that church every other day and fix things. My father is a doctor, not a handyman. And if Pastor Johnson budgeted the church's money better, he could hire a handyman and wouldn't have to worry about using too much air-conditioning on Sunday morning!"

"Your father enjoys fixing things, Alyson," my mother interjected. "Gives him something to do. Now, enough about church. Let's get that chicken and macaroni in the oven."

Edward walked into the kitchen, tossed his empty beer bottle into the trash can and grabbed another beer from the refrigerator.

"I hope you don't mind, Ma, but I invited my buddy Jackson for dinner," he said. "So we should probably set an extra place setting."

"Jasmine should be happy to hear that," said Alyson.

"Really? Why?" Edward asked.

"Yeah, why, Alyson?" I asked.

"You know why." She peered at me. "The two of them were pretty cozy the last time he was here."

Edward pointed the neck of his beer bottle toward Alyson. "You're clearly mistaken. The two of them can't stand each other. No offense, Jazzy, but he hates your guts."

"And I hate his." I almost grinned. "He's impossible to deal with."

Alyson wasn't convinced and told me so with her eyes. She gave me a look of skepticism. "We'll see."

He looked debonair in his informal blue button-down shirt, skinny khaki pants and blue casual shoes. I couldn't take my eyes off him when he first walked into the house. He gave Edward and my father a strong handshake, kissed my mother on the cheek and handed her a bottle of port.

"I wasn't sure if you drank wine, Mrs. Talbot, but I didn't want to come empty-handed this time. It'll go great with whatever dessert you have planned."

My mother checked out the label. "Thank you, sweetheart. We'll have this with our coconut cake after dinner."

"Sounds delicious." Jackson's eyes found mine as the word *delicious* drifted from his lips.

I had no time to dream about the taste of him, because my mother called us to the table.

Dinner conversation was lively with us discussing Denny's impending departure. Jackson and I seemed miles apart, but our eyes met several times during the evening. I couldn't wait to be alone with him again. I noticed that Alyson watched us like a hawk, her speculative eyes bouncing between Jackson and me throughout dinner.

Soon dinner conversation turned to that of business.

"It's not often we can get together around a table like this, so I think now's a good time to talk about the Grove and where we are with the renovation," said Edward.

"The Clydesdale is very close to completion," said Jackson. "I think you'll be very proud of what we did with it. We begin work on the Talbot House tomorrow."

"I'll definitely go by and take a look at the Clydesdale before I head to the airport tomorrow."

"We seriously need to find investors," said Alyson. "Jackson, as much as we appreciate your contribution to this project, it's not enough to sustain us in the industry. There are bigger, more elaborate resorts on Harbour Island, as you know, and we really need to be able to compete in the industry."

"I agree," said Edward. "Jasmine, how are we coming along with that business plan?"

"I'm just about there. I've done my research, and now it's just a matter of pulling it all together. And I'm also developing a solid local marketing strategy as well as a management model with policies and procedures."

"I thought we'd decided to hire a company to do all of this," said Alyson.

"No, actually, I think we decided that I would be given a chance to do it," I corrected my sister.

"Fine. But we don't have a lot of time with this. We need investors, and we can't afford to waste any time," said Alyson. "Just want to make sure you're not too distracted."

"What kind of timeline are we looking at, Jasmine?" asked Edward.

"Two weeks, tops," I said to him and then glanced at Alyson, "and I'm not distracted at all."

"Good! Then we can expect to see your final product two weeks from today," said Edward.

"I hope it's something that we can use. It would be ridiculous to waste all this time and still end up having to hire an outside company anyway," Alyson interjected.

"Jazzy's on it. If she says two weeks, then we have to give her at least that." Edward winked at me. "I have full confidence in her."

His statement meant the world to me, and I gave my brother a warm smile.

"Hey, this is supposed to be my going-away dinner. Not a business meeting," said Denny. "Can we talk about something else, please?"

"Yes." My mother stood and headed for the kitchen. "Let's talk about dessert."

After dinner we all enjoyed coconut cake and port wine on the front porch. Laughter filled the air as Edward told Sage embarrassing stories about Denny. Sage giggled as a sheepish Denny dropped his head in his hands. I found myself watching the two of them throughout the evening and smiling at the thought of their young love. I wondered if it would endure the separation they were about to experience. Would she wait for his return? Would he still want to marry Sage after he'd had his first taste of real life? In less than twenty-four hours my baby brother would be leaving the Bahamas for the first time in his life. I was afraid for him, yet proud.

Sitting on the steps, with my back against the wall, my legs stretched across the wooden porch, my feet crossed, I held on to the bowl of my wineglass. Jazz played on the stereo inside the house—it was Edward's choice of music. He was a young man, but my mother always said that he had an old soul. From the conversation, I gathered that Jackson appreciated jazz, too. Many times when I glanced over at him, his eyes were closed as he enjoyed the music.

"I really appreciate Afro-Cuban jazz artists like Jelly Roll Morton and Louis Armstrong," said Jackson. "My family is from New Orleans and much of the music there was influenced by the habanera rhythms of Cuba. Musicians from Havana and New Orleans have collaborated for years. In the early days, musicians would take an overnight ferry between the two cities to perform."

"That's interesting," said my father. "I never knew the two places had ties."

"If you've ever visited Havana…you close your eyes there and you'd swear you were in New Orleans. The ties run that deep. Not just the music, but the smells, the food, the scents from coffee," said Jackson.

"We've had many conversations about this in college," said Edward. "It's why we're such great friends. We both have a strong love for music—"

Jackson interjected, "And a yearning for information."

"A desire to know the history of things," added Edward.

"You guys are ahead of your generation. A rare breed," my father said.

"We appreciate the things that matter," said Jackson with a quick glance my way and a subtle smile.

"Jackson is quite the musician himself," said Edward, "and he sings."

"Is that true, Jackson?" my mother asked.

"Partly so, ma'am. I'm not a musician, but I do sing."

"Give us something," said Mother.

"Yeah, Jackson. Let us hear what you have," encouraged Alyson, who was working on her third glass of wine by then.

"I'm really not prepared," said Jackson, "and I don't have any music."

"He's being modest. In college, we couldn't get him to shut up," said Edward. "You don't need music. Do something a cappella."

I smiled inside, remembering how Jackson's angelic voice had sounded when he sang to me. He leaned back in his chair, crossed his leg and started to sing. As casual as the gentle breeze that subtly blew across the front porch, he belted out the words of a love song that ironically I was familiar with. John Legend's "All of Me" was a love song that the famous musician had written for his then fiancée. He spoke of loving all of her, all of her curves and edges, and all of her imperfections. I was lost in the words; the gentle melody nearly brought tears to my eyes. My heart was feeling things that my brain was having a hard time processing. I needed the two—my heart and mind—to be on one accord so that I could make sense of what I was experiencing. I fought the urge to cry and the urge to throw caution to the wind and kiss this man who seemed to be serenading me. I quickly dismissed both urges. My family would have never understood.

Alyson and my mother wiped tears from their eyes. Denny, who was holding Sage in his arms, squeezed her a bit tighter. I did the only intelligent thing—slammed the last bit of my wine, stood and walked into the house. I placed my wineglass into the sink and rushed toward my room, where I sat on the edge of my bed and let the tears flow. After I got myself together, I began to place fresh clothing into my overnight bag when strong, familiar arms wrapped themselves tightly around me.

"What's going on in that beautiful mind?" Jackson whispered part of the lyrics of the song he'd just sung.

"What are you doing in here?" I asked, glancing at the door to make sure it was shut and that no one had followed him.

"I'm falling for you," he whispered.

His lips gently kissed mine. I wrapped my arms around him and buried my face in his neck. It felt good there. Safe.

I looked into his eyes. "You need to get out of here before someone sees you."

"I'll see you at the Grove later, right?"

"Yes."

"Can't wait." He crept out of my bedroom.

I stood there for a moment, still in awe that he'd had

the nerve to come into my room. I wondered if he'd encountered anyone on the way out. But my trepidation was far outweighed by the anticipation of another night with Jackson.

At the Grove, Jackson and I sat on the back porch. Reclined on the wooden lounger, I relaxed between his legs. My back rested against his stomach, my head against his chest, and his arms held me tight. We gazed at the moon and discussed everything under the stars.

"You're still going with me to Louisiana, right?"

"Yes." I said it emphatically.

"Thank you."

He hugged me tighter, and we remained that way for most of the night.

Chapter 15

Jackson

Jasmine and I strolled down Bourbon Street arm in arm. She sipped on a hurricane from a plastic cup, while I held on to the neck of a bottle of Budweiser. Ragtime music played as we passed by souvenir shops and voodoo stores, and half-naked women danced along the street, encouraging the average passerby to come inside. I slipped a twenty-dollar bill into the hand of a homeless man who slept on the pavement. People stood on balconies above, offering green, purple and gold beads to anyone willing to flash their breasts.

"Want some beads?" I teased Jasmine.

"No, I'm good." She grinned and winked. "These babies are for your eyes only. But I will give the guys up there a little bit to dream about tonight."

She was beautiful in her baseball cap turned backward on

her head. She wore a sexy, cropped Oakland Raiders T-shirt, skinny jeans and sneakers. Men on balconies whistled and clamored, as she shook her hips to the music. She decided to give them a show, rotating her hips in a circular motion and causing a louder rumble from her male onlookers. When one of the men tossed her a set of beads, she caught them and placed them around her neck. Normally, I'd have been jealous and admonished my woman for being so brazen, but I didn't. Couldn't. I appreciated that Jasmine was gregarious and comfortable in her own skin. It was the thing that attracted me to her. It contributed to her sexiness, and I found myself rumbling with the onlookers. I knew that as much of a show as she gave them, she'd be going home with me, and me alone.

We strolled past a dimly lit nightclub, where a heavyset Aretha-Franklin-looking woman belted out her version of Marvin Gaye's "Let's Get It On." Farther down Bourbon Street, people danced to hip-hop music inside of a small space.

"Let's go inside." Jasmine pulled me toward the loud nightclub.

Strobe lights flashed across the ceiling and floors, and the smell of tobacco filled the room. The music was so loud I could barely hear myself think. We went straight for the crowded dance floor, and before I could protest we were already in the midst of the crowd, dancing to the deafening music. I wasn't much of a dancer, but I could hold my own. Jasmine, on the other hand, was a great dancer. She moved in perfect rhythm to the hip-hop sounds.

She would've danced for hours if I hadn't pulled her from the dance floor and outside for a breath of air. Not fresh air—there wasn't much fresh about the air in New Orleans, but it was air nonetheless. I was tired, on the verge of a headache, and had worked up quite an appetite.

"Let's get a bite to eat," I suggested. "We haven't eaten since breakfast at the hotel."

"I've never been to New Orleans, so I can't wait to taste the food!" she exclaimed. "What do you suggest?"

"Let's start with my favorite oyster bar," I told her. "Cooter Brown's."

I was no stranger to New Orleans, having visited there on many occasions with my family as a child. And I'd been to Mardi Gras and plenty of festivals with my college buddies. It was nothing for us to catch a flight to the Crescent City on a Friday afternoon and make it back just in time for Monday morning classes. Hungover and exhausted, we were satisfied that we'd had the best time of our lives.

"Raw oysters?" She frowned.

"On a half shell," I said as if that made them more appealing. "You'll love them."

"I can't imagine that I will."

"Girl, you eat pigeon peas and rice. What could be worse than that?"

"At least it's cooked."

"Where's your audacity?" I asked her the same question she'd recently asked me.

"You can't use my words," she said. "Get your own!"

I dismissed her grumblings, grabbed her hand and led the way to Cooter Brown's, a favorite of the locals, where they served some of the largest oysters in town. It was a casual spot with big-screen televisions and a pool table. The most coveted spot in the house was at the bar, and we were lucky enough to snag a couple of seats. We ordered a dozen oysters and I quickly downed one as I handed Jasmine one. She frowned and held it between her thumb and index finger, her pinkie finger sticking out as if she was sipping tea in England.

"You gotta get dirty with it, baby. You can't hold it like

that…all prim and proper." I squeezed lime juice onto her oyster and sprinkled it with a bit of hot sauce. "Now toss it into your mouth."

She slurped the oyster from its shell and chewed. Her frown slowly changed. "It's not so bad."

"That's right!" I yelled over the loud conversations. "What you drinking?"

"You order for me!" she yelled.

"A couple of Coronas," I ordered and then told the shucker, "Give us another dozen!"

We ate raw oysters on the half shell, drank beers and laughed together. I had fun with Jasmine. She was like no other woman I'd ever been with, and she was slowly conquering my heart. We finished our beers and the second dozen oysters and then stepped out into the star-filled night, where we strolled down the street toward our hotel in the French Quarter. A good night's sleep was in the plans because tomorrow would be a big day.

"Are you nervous about meeting him?" Jasmine asked.

"Yeah, a little." It was a lie. I wasn't a little nervous, but a lot.

I grabbed her hand as we walked through the lobby of our hotel and took the elevator up to the twenty-seventh floor. As we walked into our suite, I tossed the room key onto the coffee table and flipped on the television set.

"I'm going to slip into something more comfortable," said Jasmine.

As she disappeared into the bedroom, and then into the shower, I stretched my long legs across the sofa in the living area, tuned the television to ESPN and caught highlights of the game on SportsCenter. Sensual, fragrant smells slid from beneath the cracks in the door and swept across my nostrils. I heard the shower cut off. I watched as Jasmine pranced across the floor of the bedroom in a sheer, sexy nightie. I shut off the television and went into the bedroom.

"Very nice." I smiled.

"Thank you," she said and modeled her lingerie. "Just a little something I picked up at the mall earlier today."

"Were you and I at the same mall? Because I don't remember that little nightie."

"I purchased it when you slipped away to the jewelry store."

"Oh, you mean the jewelry store where I picked this up." I pulled a blue velvet box out of one of the pockets of my sweats, opened it and pulled out the diamond necklace I'd chosen for Jasmine earlier in the day.

I saw so many things that I wanted for her, but I needed to keep things light and unclouded. I wanted Jasmine to love me for me, not for the things that I could provide for her. She had been in relationships before where she used men as a tool to get what she wanted or needed. I wouldn't be that guy. I would give her the world, but only after I knew that she loved me without consequence.

I placed the necklace around her neck.

"Jackson, it's beautiful."

"I know," I teased her, "and there's more where that came from, but you have to work for it."

"Excuse me?"

"Yeah." I smiled. "What did you think this was?"

I grabbed her small waist and pulled her close. She gently caressed my face with her soft hands. I kissed her forehead and her nose, nibbled on her neck and then gently kissed her lips.

"I'm going to hop in the shower," I told her and pulled myself away to rush into the bathroom.

I stood beneath the water and thought about the morning ahead of me. Though just a few miles away, the drive from New Orleans to the city where my biological father served as mayor would be the longest drive of my life. I'd pieced together my speech and rehearsed my lines a thousand times. He was up for reelection, so the news might cause some concern for him. But I was confident that a man of his stature could handle most anything.

According to my research, Patrick H. Wells had been married to the same woman, Marjorie, for almost forty years. There were two children from their union. Patrick Jr. was a graduate of Louisiana State University and was interning as an assistant at his father's office. His daughter, Leslie, was currently attending Xavier. Mayor Wells served as Head Deacon of his conservative Methodist church in New Orleans. He lived in a prominent community and was well connected. And according to a magazine article I'd read, his family was compared to the television family the Cosbys: educated, professional, successful—not one blemish. They were a perfect family in the eyes of society.

I didn't need his prominence or his connections. I wasn't seeking to be included in his will or to be compensated in any way. I simply needed to fill this void that suddenly lingered in my life. I needed to satisfy my curiosity about the man who was my father. I wanted to be accepted by him and his children—my siblings—and possibly build a relationship with them. I wanted to know what he would've done had he known that I existed. Would he have been a part of my life? Would I have spent summers and holidays in Louisiana with him and his family? Would his marriage have ended because of my mother or because of me? I had so many questions, and I fully intended to have them answered very soon.

I stepped out of the shower, wrapped the plush towel around my waist. When I glanced at my face in the mirror, it was the same face I'd seen on the internet—Patrick H.

Wells's face. The resemblance was remarkable. He wouldn't be able to deny the truth. But would he accept it? I hoped he didn't suffer from hypertension, because I knew the moment I walked into his City Hall office in the morning, my presence might send his blood pressure to new heights.

I walked into the bedroom, anxious to get back to the beautiful woman lying in my bed. She was curled up on the bed, a sheet covering her hips and light snores escaping from her lips. It seemed I'd spent too much time in the shower.

I watched her for a moment, stared at her beauty. She had suddenly appeared in my life and had begun to rearrange my feelings. I wanted to hear her voice and see her face daily. And when we were apart, I missed her as if she'd been in my life for a significant amount of time. And I counted the moments until I'd see her again.

I pulled the sheet up to her chest, gave her a gentle kiss on the cheek and turned off the bedside light. Then I went into the other room and found SportsCenter again.

Jasmine and I took the elevator to the seventh floor. City Hall was busy as any governmental office would be on a Monday morning. I'd chosen my best suit, the navy one, complete with cuff links and my perfectly shined wing-tip oxfords. Jasmine's professional look intrigued me. I was convinced that she would be gorgeous in whatever she decided to wear, and she was. Carrying my portfolio in my arms, we strode through the glass doors of the mayor's office. I had scheduled the appointment, pretending that I wanted to discuss plans for a new development project that the mayor had been passionate about. He was more than anxious to speak with me about it.

"Good morning, Mr. Conner. Mayor Wells will be with

you momentarily," said his personal secretary. "You look oddly familiar."

"You think so?" I asked.

She stood there for a moment, trying to place where she knew me. "Can I get you something to drink? Coffee or water?"

"No, ma'am. I'm fine, thank you."

Jasmine declined anything as well, and we both took a seat on the brown leather sofa in the waiting area. My leg bounced up and down from nervousness. I looked at Jasmine and she offered me a calming smile. She'd already given me a pep talk on the way over in our rented vehicle. She'd held my hand and vowed to support me every step of the way. I believed her.

"The mayor will see you now, Mr. Conner," the secretary said and ushered us into the mayor's office.

I was taken aback by the view from his office. It was breathtaking, with an enormous window that overlooked the city. The office was huge, with a mahogany desk and a sitting area with plush leather furniture. His back to us, he faced the window while he finished a phone call. When he spun around in his chair to face us, he looked as if he'd seen a ghost, and I felt as if I'd seen one, too. The face was very similar to the one I'd seen in the mirror.

I wondered if Patrick H. Wells was as excited to see me as I was him. All night I'd stayed awake, staring at the ceiling, contemplating this meeting. I had rehearsed my lines carefully—pondered what I wanted to say to my father when I met him for the first time. I was prepared, I thought. Hell, I'd been through worse things. However, I hadn't anticipated the anxiety that I would feel once I laid eyes on him. Nothing could've prepared me for that. My heart pounded a mile a minute, and my palms began to sweat.

"Yes. Yes, Dan. I'll have Gloria draw up the memo the moment I hang up," he said to the person on the other end of the phone. "You can count on it. Yep. All right. Goodbye."

He stood and came around from behind his desk. Jasmine and I both stood, and he gave us each a strong handshake before we sat back down.

"Mr. Conner. Good to meet you."

"Good to meet you, too, Mayor."

"I'm anxious to hear about your plans for the city's recovery project. It's one of my priorities. The city hasn't fully recovered from Katrina, but we're on an upward stride," he stated.

"Yes, we are, sir. I'm familiar with some of your initiatives for rebuilding the city. However, I have to be honest with you. I'm not here to discuss the city's recovery project."

"You're not?"

"No, sir." I took a deep breath. "I'm here on a more personal matter."

"And what matter would that be?"

"My mother is Sarah Conner."

"Sarah Conner?" He pretended not to recall who my mother was.

"Sarah Conner that you worked with on the Democratic campaign in the eighties. The beautiful woman that you had an affair with." I had to state it that way because he was still giving me a look of confusion.

"Ah, Sarah." He leaned back in his chair and smiled a little at the remembrance.

"Did you know that when you and she parted ways, she was pregnant?"

"No, I didn't. But what does that have to do with me?"

"She was pregnant with me, and I'm your son."

Patrick H. Wells stood, paced the floor. He was in shock. He took a deep breath. "Who told you that?"

"My mother told me that."

I could see that he was uncomfortable and his mind raced to process the information. "What is this, some sort of joke?"

"It's the truth."

"Sarah sent you here?" he asked. "What is it that she wants from me? Is it money?"

"I'm sure she doesn't want anything from you."

"Then why would you come here after all these years and bring this up?"

"In my warped and twisted mind, I thought somehow… you might be happy to see me."

"If I were to believe for one second that you were my son," Patrick H. Wells said, "I would have to ask what it is that you want from me."

"I don't want anything from you. I simply wanted to know who you were, so that I could have peace in my own life."

"Did my opponent dig you and your mother up from under a rock to jeopardize my campaign? Everyone knows that I'm up for reelection, and only a few people knew about my dealings with Sarah."

"I don't give a damn about your reelection. My mother told me that you are my father and I wanted to come see you for myself. I thought you might want to know that you had a son out there. Thought you might be happy to know that."

"Do you understand who I am? Not only am I a public figure, but I've been happily married for almost forty years…"

"Yes, I know. I read it on the internet. Marjorie, right?"

"This would kill her," said Wells. "My wife is not well."

"I'm not trying to hurt your wife or your campaign or any of that. I came because I wanted to meet the man who I recently found out was my biological father. I wanted to see you for myself. I thought that if I met you, I would somehow feel free and complete."

"Were you expecting me to be overjoyed by this news, son?"

"I don't know what I was expecting," I said, "but certainly not this."

"How do I even know with any certainty that you are my son?"

"Because I look just like your ass!" I stood and grabbed Jasmine's hand. "Let's go."

"This would ruin my career. It would ruin everything that I've worked hard for. Can't you see that? If the media gets ahold of this, I won't even be considered for another term. The folks in my district are conservative. They won't understand this. My family wouldn't understand."

"My mother didn't want me to come, and now I see why. I have no idea what she ever saw in you. Good day, sir."

"I won't let you ruin me," he managed to say before I slammed the door in his face.

I didn't leave the meeting feeling free at all. In fact, I felt all but free. Somehow I'd thought the reunion would end more favorably and that the feelings that had caused my turmoil would go away. But they didn't, and I had a new set of feelings. Unfamiliar ones. I felt rejected, disrespected, and wanted to punch something. I thought of punching the silver elevator doors, but didn't want to risk being hauled off to jail.

"At least you know what a jerk he is." Jasmine tried to ease the pain, but nothing she said helped.

"I don't know why I came here," I spat.

I drove quickly through the side streets and hopped onto

the interstate, heading straight for the airport as fast as I could get us there. I was silent in the car and the whole trip back to the Bahamas. I wondered how long it would take me to recover from this. I just didn't know.

Chapter 16

Jasmine

"Are you going to the Grove tonight?"

"No."

I tried again. "I was thinking about spending the night there. Maybe broil a couple of steaks, baked potatoes, open a bottle of merlot."

"I'm going to my hotel."

"You have to eat, Jackson. You haven't eaten a thing all day. Maybe we can stop over at Ma Ruby's for a burger or something."

"Not hungry." He sat in the back of the taxi with his arms folded across his chest. It was the first time we'd spoken since our flight left Louis Armstrong New Orleans International Airport.

"Maybe I can come to your hotel with you." I was grasping at straws. I hated the way I felt at the moment; it reminded me of the old Jasmine—the one who'd gravitated toward toxic relationships with men who couldn't have cared less about me. It was hurtfully familiar.

"I just want to be alone." His words pierced my heart. He addressed the taxi driver. "Take me to the Coral Sands Hotel, please."

The driver did exactly that. When we pulled up in front of the hotel, Jackson stepped out of the cab and handed the driver the fare.

"Please take her to the Grove. It's in Dunmore Town. She can direct you there," he said to the driver and then stuck his head inside the back window of the cab. "I'll see you tomorrow, Jasmine."

"Are you kidding, Jackson?" I asked. "That's all you have to say—*I'll see you tomorrow, Jasmine*?"

"What else would you like for me to say?"

"Talk to me! Tell me what you're thinking, feeling. I'm here for you," I pleaded and then attempted to whisper. "Don't just dismiss me like this."

I watched as the driver peered at me through the rearview mirror.

"I don't know what I'm feeling or thinking. I just know that I need some time to sort things out."

"Okay," I mumbled and then stared out the window. Tears threatened to burn my eyes, but I willed them away. "Fine."

I heard the car door slam and was suddenly grateful that he was gone.

As we pulled away from the hotel, I told the driver, "Take me to the water ferry, please."

On the drive to the ferry, I looked down at my phone. Hoped to receive a call or text from Jackson. Wished he'd had a change of heart or at least an apology, but my phone hadn't rung, and there were no text messages.

I needed to go home. I needed to see my father. Needed him to help me make sense of things.

When I got there, I found Daddy relaxing on the front porch, his legs crossed and a copy of the Eleutheran newspaper hiding his face. The cabdriver lifted my luggage out of the trunk and I rolled it up the sidewalk.

"Going somewhere or just returning?" Daddy asked.

"Returning."

I left my suitcase at the bottom of the stairs and took a seat next to my father.

"Where you been?" he asked and then folded the paper into his lap.

"New Orleans," I told him.

"Sweet New Orleans," he said with a smile, "the Crescent City."

"With Jackson."

"Ah. The contractor fellow. The guy you've been gallivanting about town with."

"How did you know?"

"I've been around the block a time or two. You can't get much past your old man, sweetheart," he said. "Why is your heart heavy?"

"Jackson went to Louisiana looking for his biological father, and when he found him, the man all but threw us out of his office."

"I see."

"And Jackson was so hurt and bothered by it that he stopped speaking to me. He barely said anything to me the whole way back to the Bahamas. Do you know how long a trip it is from New Orleans to Eleuthera?" I asked. "I have done nothing!"

"People deal with pain in different ways, Jazzy. Maybe he just needs a little space."

"Well, I intend to give him a lot of space! I don't even

know why I put myself out there again. Do I have the words *vulnerable* or *desperate* written across my forehead?"

"No, you don't."

"Then what's wrong with me, Dad? Why do men make it their business to mistreat me?"

"I think you might be overreacting a bit, sweetheart. Being rejected is a hard thing for a man. And being rejected by a father is even harder. Maybe the man just needs a little time to sort things out."

"Maybe." I stood. "I'm going to find something to eat and take a shower. The business plan is complete, but I want to put the finishing touches on the Grove's marketing plan."

"Congratulations for getting that done. I'm proud of you," he said. "Leave your bag. I'll bring it inside."

"Thanks, Daddy." I kissed my father's cheek and then headed inside.

After a long, relaxing shower, I locked myself in my room. Turned on a little Beres Hammond and then searched for my laptop. I figured my father must've forgotten to bring it inside. I found Daddy in the kitchen, his legs extending from beneath the sink and a wrench grasped tightly in his hands. He was attempting to repair the kitchen sink.

"Daddy?"

He bumped his head on the cabinet as he stuck his head out to look at me. "What's going on, sweetheart?"

"Did you bring my laptop in with my other bags?"

"Didn't see your laptop. Only the luggage on wheels."

"Well, it was with the other bag."

"Nope, just one bag, sweetheart. You only had one when you got out of the cab."

"Are you sure?"

"Quite sure."

"Shit!" I said. "I mean shoot! Sorry, Daddy."

He chuckled and then popped his head back underneath the sink. My father had no earthly idea that my entire life was on that laptop. Everything that meant anything to me was all there. My photos, music, documents—very private documents. And moreover, the Grove's business and marketing plans and all the hard work I'd put into them were now floating around somewhere. There was no way I would be able to reproduce them in such a short period of time.

I needed to retrace my steps and figure out where I'd misplaced my life. I didn't remember having my laptop on the plane. The last time I remembered seeing it was at the hotel. Or maybe it was in the rental car. Perhaps I had it when we went to the mayor's office. I couldn't be certain of anything. Dealing with Jackson's grief had me out of sorts, and I was quickly coming unglued. Without that business plan, I would be a failure in the eyes of my siblings forever. They would never trust me again. And I knew it.

Chapter 17

Jackson

I was consumed with the Grove. My goal was to complete this project well ahead of schedule, and at the rate I was working my men, we would accomplish just that. I had gotten off course—allowed Jasmine to distract me, and I needed to refocus. Additionally, I needed to wipe any memory of Patrick H. Wells from my mind. I wanted to forget that I'd ever met the man, and in order to do that I had to immerse myself in my work. Work became my refuge.

When my phone rang, I barely heard my Jay-Z ringtone.

"Edward, what's up?" I answered.

"Fantastic news," he said. Edward was never one to shoot the breeze or engage in meaningless small talk. He was a straight shooter: always got right to the point. "We have a potential investor!"

"Wow. Really?"

"Darren Spencer is an old family friend," Edward said.

I became uneasy at the sound of Jasmine's ex-boyfriend's name. I was jealous, no doubt, but hoped that Edward didn't hear it in my voice.

"As a matter of fact, he and Jasmine dated in high school. So we've known the Spencers for a long time. They're very wealthy, and they might be interested in investing in the Grove. No doubt, in the past there was a bit of contention between the two families, but I'm hopeful that we can move past it and do business together..."

My mind went back to when Jasmine took me past Darren's former home. I was uncomfortable then, and I was uncomfortable now as Edward continued to talk about Jasmine's ex-boyfriend.

"...with their experience in the hospitality industry, they not only can offer funding, but expertise. Not to mention they're Bahamian. Maybe Darren could even help bring Jasmine up to speed on some of the day-to-day stuff. Maybe they'll even fall in love again. I hear that he's on the outs with his wife." Edward laughed. "I'm waiting for Jasmine to send me that business plan so that I can take a look at it before we send it over to them. Have you seen her at the Grove?"

"Not in a couple of days. No."

"My parents said she's been staying at the Clydesdale. I'm surprised you haven't run into her."

It was true. I hadn't run into Jasmine in a couple of days. Not since New Orleans. Partly because she'd been avoiding me, and I hadn't gone looking for her either. I was embarrassed about my behavior the day we returned from Louisiana, and I didn't quite know how to make things right. She stayed locked in her office for the better part of each day, and I barely even caught a glimpse of her.

"I haven't really been to the Clydesdale since we've completed the work over there."

"Right," he said, "okay. Look, man, if you happen to bump into her, can you have her give me a call?"

"Will do, bro."

"The Spencers will be on Harbour Island next week. I'd like to have that business and marketing plan to them by the weekend," he said. "Also, when they get there, I'd like for you to give them a grand tour of the Grove…show them the Clydesdale and share our vision for the other two houses."

"Absolutely. Consider it done."

"Thanks, man. I feel really positive about this."

"That's awesome," I said, "and if I bump into Jasmine, I'll have her call you."

"Cool. Talk to you soon."

He was gone. And now I had to face Jasmine. The truth was, I felt her absence, missed her presence, but didn't know how to approach her. I told myself that I just needed a few days of space, but a few days had turned into much more than I wanted or expected. Things were awkward now. I wanted her to know that she hadn't done anything wrong. It was me—not her.

I knocked on the door of her office.

"Yes?"

I opened the door without responding. Our eyes met, and I realized just how much I missed her beautiful face.

"Hey," I said.

She was all business, no affection. "How can I help you?"

"How you doing?"

"I'm fine." She didn't look fine. She looked fatigued. She gave me a look of impatience.

"I haven't really seen you around lately. Just wanted to say hello. See how you're doing."

"I'm doing great. Was there something you needed?"

"Just…um…" She threw me off with her cold demeanor. "Edward has been trying to reach you. He wants you to give him a call."

"Okay." She looked at me as if to say, "Is that all?"

"He wants to know how you're coming with the business plan."

"Not very well, considering I lost my laptop somewhere between here and the state of Louisiana and can't even begin to tell you where it might be. My business and marketing plans are lost somewhere. So do me a favor and tell my older brother and sister that they were both right about me all along. I'm a total failure, and they should've hired an outside company."

"You're not a failure, Jasmine. You're a bright, capable woman."

"Really?" she asked sarcastically. "If I'm so bright and capable, why don't I have anything to show for all of my hard work? And why do I keep inviting toxic men into my life who are only interested in climbing into my bed, and once they've gotten what they want, they move on?"

It was apparent she had a lot on her mind. It was as if she'd been waiting for the perfect time to unload it all on me.

"Are you referring to me?"

"If the shoe fits."

"First off, I think we both climbed into that bed together. And we each put ourselves out there," I said, trying to explain my position, "and I haven't moved on. I'm right here."

"That's funny because you haven't been right anywhere since we left Louisiana. In fact, I've barely seen your face in days. Haven't heard two words from you. Which is crazy, especially since I had no earthly reason whatsoever to go to Louisiana. I only went to support you!"

"I appreciate that. I just needed some space. Some time to absorb things."

"Well, hopefully I've given you ample *space* to absorb things." She dismissed me with her eyes and went back to typing on her computer. "Now if you'll excuse me, I have work to do."

I opened my mouth to protest or explain. I didn't know what to say. It was too late. I'd blown it with her. I shut her door and stood on the other side for a few moments—thinking about what I should've said or what I could go back in and say. So many thoughts raced through my head. I pulled her door open again.

"Jasmine, I'm sorry. I never meant to hurt you."

"Well, you did," she said.

"I hope you can find it in your heart to forgive me," I said and then pulled her door closed again.

My heart ached for her. I hoped I hadn't lost her for good. My heart wanted to fight for us, but my mind said we were better off this way. I sighed and then headed out the front door. I told myself that my life was much less complicated without a woman in it. Especially a complicated woman like Jasmine Talbot.

I walked over to the Talbot House. The work there was midway complete. The linoleum had been removed and the original hardwoods refinished, the wiring and electrical done, the walls primed. The Talbot House required more work than the Clydesdale had and demanded more of my time and attention to the project, which worked out perfectly. I worked long hours and weekends and literally collapsed into bed every night. And tonight would be no different. In fact, I looked forward to my comfortable hotel bed.

"Everybody's going to the fish fry tonight. You game?" Lance asked as he came up to me. He was filthy, with dust all over his face and clothing.

"Nah, I have other plans. Maybe next time."

"What plans?"

"I'm going over to Ma Ruby's and grabbing one of those world-renowned burgers to go and a Bahamian beer. I'm going to step into the shower, eat and crash."

"Sounds boring," said Lance. "Not hooking up with Jasmine?"

I had never discussed Jasmine with Lance or the other guys, but obviously they knew that something had gone on between us. Over the past several weeks and long before the New Orleans trip, there had been an apparent change in my attitude, and I'd become less of a workaholic and more carefree.

"We all know about you and Jasmine," Lance said when I didn't respond.

"Really?" I asked.

"Yes. Neither of you are very good at sneaking around together."

"I really don't want this to change how we do business with the Talbots. If her brother Edward knew, he might not understand...and I really need this gig. I have a lot invested."

"Hey, bro. It's me, Lance. We're friends, remember? I wouldn't do anything to jeopardize your livelihood or mine, for that matter. I'm actually a little pissed that you didn't tell me the truth. I had to figure it out on my own." He silenced his ringing phone. "I thought we were better than that."

"We *are* better than that."

"I mean, I was right there when Denise ripped your heart out and squashed it with the heel of her stiletto."

"She didn't quite rip my heart out."

"What would you call it?"

"We had a misunderstanding," I said. "Now, exactly how much do you know about me and Jasmine?"

"I know about the late nights at the Grove. I know that she's transformed you into someone I don't recognize. You're much happier and very mellow. At least you were. I know that she accompanied you on that trip to Louisiana, but the two of you haven't talked much since. Did something happen?"

"I'm just dealing with my own crap, man. It has nothing to do with her."

"Well, I hope you work it out. Jasmine is as sweet as can be. Not to mention gorgeous with a knockout body. She's funny, she can cook and she's managed to change you in a very short time."

"I think I love her." I caught myself by surprise with the admission of it. I loved Jasmine. I couldn't remember ever feeling this way about anyone before now.

"What did you say? Can you repeat that? I don't think I heard you right." Lance pressed his hand against his ear.

"You heard me right." I said.

"Wow, that's a huge thing for Jackson Conner to admit. I don't think I've ever heard you say that about anyone."

"I've never felt that about anyone."

"Jax, man, I haven't seen you happy in a long time. I hope it works out for you, buddy."

"I don't know. I think she hates me now."

"I doubt that. You're a great guy, but whatever the hell you did to her you need to swallow your pride and make it right," he said. "She's one of the good ones. You don't want to lose her."

"You're right."

"I know I am. Good luck with that." He reached for a

handshake. "If you change your mind about the fish fry, you know where to find us."

I nodded and shook Lance's hand.

I pulled out my cell phone and called Tracy.

"I need your help," I told her. "I need you to locate a laptop. It's somewhere between here and Louisiana."

Tracy was the most resourceful person I knew. If Jasmine's laptop could be found, Tracy would certainly be the one to find it.

After work as I caught a taxi to the Coral Sands Hotel, I decided that I didn't want my night to end just yet. I showered and changed into a pair of jeans and a casual shirt. Then I made my way to Governor's Harbour. At the very least I could have a bite to eat and beer with my buddies at the island's fish fry. It was something to do—something to take my mind off of everything.

Caribbean music played beneath the moonlit sky. Bahamian natives prepared fresh fish, and hot grills were fired up along the sand. Men, women and children danced to Caribbean rhythms. I found Lance and the others gathered around a table, enjoying the island fare and sipping on Bahamian brews. I grabbed a seat at the table.

"Mr. Conner!" Jorge was the first to shake my hand.

"Hey, let's get him caught up," said Diego as he rushed to the bar. He came back with two beers and handed them both to me. "You've got a long way to go."

I twisted the cap off one of the bottles and we toasted.

"To the Grove!" said Lance and we all cheered as our bottles clanked together.

"To the Grove," I said, taking a long gulp. I needed it.

But after a few beers, I abandoned the crowd and went for a stroll along the beach. I needed to clear my head. No matter how I tried to drown my feelings, my heart ached

and I missed Jasmine. She had been nothing but supportive to me and I'd hurt her. She hadn't deserved my cold
shoulder. I kept replaying our conversation in my mind—
the one earlier that day at the Grove. She'd referred to me
as toxic and compared me to other men in her life. Her
words still stung. *"I had no earthly reason whatsoever to
go to Louisiana. I only went to support you!"*

She was right.

My phone rang and I hoped it was Jasmine. I needed
to hear her voice. It took a moment to retrieve it from the
pocket of my jeans.

"I found it!" Tracy's voice couldn't contain her excite-
ment and pride. "I'm having the laptop delivered by mes-
senger tomorrow."

"Are you kidding?"

"Dead serious," she said. "You owe me big-time!"

"Where was it?"

"At the New Orleans hotel where you and—" she cleared
her throat "—the *missus* spent the night. I won't even ask
who the *missus* is."

"I'll tell you all about her soon enough," I said. "But
when I called, the hotel told us they hadn't found a missing laptop. Gave us the runaround about it."

"They just needed their memory refreshed a bit."

"Thank you so much, Tracy. I don't know how to repay
you."

"Well, I have an idea. There's a teenage boy at my house
who needs a male voice in his ear. You can start there."

"Consider it done," I told her. "I have tickets to the
next Miami Heat home game. Maybe Devante and I can
check it out."

"He would die if I told him!"

"Then don't tell him. Let's make it a surprise."

"Thanks, Jackson."

"No, thank you for finding that laptop. You can't imagine how much it means to me."

"Glad I could help."

When I hung up, I wanted to do a Toyota jump. I was excited that Jasmine's laptop had been located, and I couldn't wait to tell her. Hopefully this would make things right between us again—perhaps she'd even forgive me for being an ass.

Chapter 18

Jasmine

Edward and Alyson looked like census takers as they walked around the outside of the property. Dressed in bureaucratic-looking suits and carrying briefcases, they would've been mistaken for a couple of bill collectors if I hadn't known any better. I wanted to run and hide before they made their way inside the Clydesdale, but there was nowhere to escape to. So I stood in the doorway and smiled as they approached.

They were in awe of the work that had been completed thus far. The Clydesdale was fully furnished with antique furnishings, many of which were restored pieces that belonged to our grandparents. Aside from the Grand Room that housed my grandfather's grand piano, the Clydesdale's kitchen had been converted into a commercial space, fully stocked with stainless-steel appliances. The rustic table in the dining room would be a place where guests would gather for Bahamian meals during their stay. Each of the five bedrooms in the Clydesdale had its own name and a separate theme. The Symonette Room had already become my personal favorite. With a view of the ocean, it was the largest and most lavish room, decorated with a canopy bed, and it would no doubt be our most lucrative room. The Goombay overlooked the flower garden and had been my temporary office. The Junkanoo boasted bright colors, as festive as the event that it was named after. The Blake and the Sweet Emily were the smaller two rooms, both bursting with character. The newly built patio with a fully stocked bar would be the perfect place for patrons to spend their evenings gazing at the stars while enjoying a rum punch or sky juice.

I followed my siblings upstairs as they toured the house.

"What brings you here today?" I asked the obvious.

They were there to retrieve and review copies of my business and marketing plans. Plans that I'd lost somewhere in Louisiana and hadn't been able to reproduce. The truth was inevitable. And it was best that they knew it sooner than later.

"It's been two weeks, Jasmine," said Alyson. She was all business. "You know why we're here."

Edward gave me a hug and a kiss on the cheek. "Things are really looking good around here."

"It really does look great," said Alyson. "Jackson Conner does good work."

"This has far exceeded my expectations," said Edward. "I'm just in awe. And I can't wait to see what he does with the other two houses."

"The Talbot House is just about completed as well," I added. Why was I stalling the inevitable with small talk?

"I'd like to get that business plan over to the Spencers this afternoon. That'll give them a couple of days to review it before our meeting," said Edward as he looked at the ceiling fan and fixtures in the Goombay Room. "So, where is it?"

"There's been an unfortunate delay…" I said. "Um…I don't really know how to tell you this…but…"

"I knew it! You couldn't do it," said Alyson matter-of-factly. "I told Edward on the flight over here that we were crazy not to hire a company to do this. Now here we are two days away from a meeting with potential investors, and we don't have a business plan."

Before I could respond, I heard the front door open and close, then heavy footsteps up the stairs. I started to call out when Jackson walked into the room. He carried a laptop in his hands that resembled mine and a manila folder. What was happening?

"I know you asked me to have five copies printed up, but I was only able to print three," he said and handed me the manila folder. "The copies were just delivered by courier."

I gave him a look of confusion. I had no earthly idea what he was talking about.

"Is that Jasmine's business plan?" asked Edward.

"Yes, it is. She asked me to give it a quick review before she turned it over to you guys." Jackson gave me a wink. "And I have to say…I wasn't able to review the entire plan, but the parts I read were…phenomenal."

They were? I could hardly believe what my ears were hearing. And where had Jackson found my laptop?

"May I?" Edward reached for a copy.

Jackson handed him one and then Alyson.

"We'll need to give it a good review before we even think about sending it over to the Spencers," said Alyson.

I gave Jackson my *what's-going-on* face, and he handed me the third copy. I flipped through the crisp white pages.

With just a quick review, I knew that it was, in fact, my business plan. Then he handed me my laptop and I was even more confused.

"This is very well put together," said Edward. "I'm going to spend the rest of the day going over it. I'd like to get it to the Spencers by this afternoon. Can you send me an electronic copy of this?"

"Of course," I said.

"I'm proud of you, Jazzy. You've done good," said Edward.

"I'm surprised," Alyson added.

"We're headed over to Governor's Harbour. Mother has enticed us with breakfast and we're definitely going to take her up on it." Edward asked, "Care to join us?"

"No. I've got some things I need to finish up here."

"It's Saturday!" exclaimed Edward. "Saturday is your day to shop."

"Not anymore. Not since the Grove has evolved. I have a checklist a mile long and a strict timeline."

"Don't become a workaholic like this guy." Edward slapped his hand against Jackson's chest. "The two of you are becoming a lot alike."

"Aren't they?" asked Alyson.

"Well, if you won't join us for breakfast we'll see you this afternoon," said Edward.

"I'll be right here." I followed them down the stairs and walked them to the door and couldn't wait for them to exit. "Tell Ma to save me a bowl of fish stew."

"Will do," said Edward.

As the two of them slipped into the backseat of a taxicab, I finally exhaled.

I turned to Jackson and the questions spewed out. "What was that? Where did you find my laptop? How did you find my laptop? When did you have copies of my business plan printed?"

He responded by locking his lips with mine. I was still confused, but simply relaxed in his arms and enjoyed the kiss. Oh, how I missed those lips, his touch.

"Forgive me," he whispered.

"Forgiven," I whispered back. "You just saved my butt."

"You're welcome," he said.

"Thank you."

"Did it get me back into your good graces?" he asked.

"Big-time," I told him. "How did you manage to find the laptop?"

"My assistant is very resourceful and was able to pull some strings. She made it happen."

"You should give her my regards."

"I will," he told me. "So I can see you later, then? Maybe take you to dinner or for a walk along the beach?"

"Maybe both."

"I can't be without you again, Jasmine. It's too painful. I need you."

I was speechless. I couldn't remember ever being needed before. My heart was overjoyed.

"Get out of here, please. Do you know what people would say if they walked in here and saw me in your arms and our lips locked together?"

"They would say, 'Now, that's one lucky bastard right there. He must be in love with her and doesn't care who knows it.'"

"Love?"

"Yes, love," he said. "I wasn't sure at first, but now I'm pretty certain."

"What makes you so certain now?" I couldn't help but blush.

"For starters, I think about you all the time—way too

often. I have a strong desire to be with you every moment of every day. I need to see your beautiful face and hear your voice. I'm lost when we're apart," he said. "Even my staff has noticed a difference in me."

"They know about us?"

"I'm afraid they do," said Jackson.

"My father knows, too," I told him.

"You told your daddy about me?" he asked with a smirk.

"Everything."

"Everything?" Jackson asked. "Is he looking for me?"

"Quite possibly."

We both laughed heartily.

"Thank you for having my back today," I said. "I can't even begin to tell you how much that meant to me."

"You don't have to tell me, because I already know," he said. "I will always have your back, Jasmine. I promise."

"That's a huge promise," I told him.

"I always keep my promises."

I placed my hand gently on his face. "I'm going to hold you to it."

After a quick kiss on my nose, Jackson held me tightly. Neither of us wanted to let go.

"I've come up with the perfect way that you can repay me for saving your butt today."

"How?" I asked.

"Miami Heat versus the LA Lakers, center court seats, Friday night. You, me, a hormonal teenage boy and nachos."

"What?"

"Just pack a weekend bag, and be ready for an afternoon flight to Key West and an adventurous drive to Miami… *and*…my mother's going to love you," said Jackson. "Trust me."

Before I could protest or ask the million questions that

suddenly raced through my head, Jackson kissed my lips and then rushed out the door.

Saturdays had begun to feel just like weekdays since the Clydesdale was completed, and the Talbot House wasn't far behind. The Grove was beginning to feel like a real business. There was so much that needed to be done. Applications for operational licenses and permits needed to be followed up on. Governmental agencies needed to be consulted. An accountant needed to be hired soon, and the Grove's staffing plan needed to be executed.

I was happy to have my laptop back and intact. All my files and pictures were in place and hadn't been tampered with. I sat down in my chair and decided to check my email. I was surprised to find an email from my brother Edward to Charles Spencer—Darren's father—with a copy to me. My business plan had been attached without any changes or additions. My name had been given as a point of contact in case there were questions. I had successfully earned my brother's trust and quite possibly my sister's. I wasn't so sure how much of Alyson's trust I had earned, but I really didn't care. I'd earned Edward's and that was all that mattered. It felt good. On top of it, Jackson was in love with me—and I with him. Life was golden again.

Chapter 19

Jasmine

Darren was a mirror image of his father, Charles Spencer. Both men were handsome, tall, with dark skin and medium build. The only visible difference was the elder Spencer's graying beard. As much as I hated to admit it, Darren looked dazzling in his executive, navy suit. I couldn't help but stare. With a precise haircut and a perfectly shaven face, he was more handsome than I remembered. And when he hugged me, I remembered how those arms felt around me.

"Hello, Jasmine," he said in his Bahamian dialect. "You look fantastic."

"Thanks. So do you."

"It's been too long." Darren grabbed my hands, opened my arms wide to get a better look at me. "You're still as beautiful as ever."

Jackson stood in the corner of the room, his arms folded across his chest. It was obvious that he was uncomfortable with the attention that Darren showed me. Alyson offered her own look of disapproval and rolled her eyes.

"Why don't we all have a seat in the dining room," Edward suggested.

Alyson had already snagged the seat at the head of the table. Darren and his father followed Edward into the dining room. I took a seat at the table opposite of Darren, and Jackson took the seat next to me.

"Jasmine, I understand that you were the one to prepare the business and marketing plan," said Mr. Spencer. He looked distinguished in his gray suit, and his smile, though rarely seen, was much more gorgeous than his son's.

"Yes, sir."

"It was surprisingly very well put together," he said. *Surprisingly.*

"Thank you, sir." I said it even though I felt disrespected in that moment.

"Where have you worked since college?"

Edward attempted to divert Mr. Spencer's impending line of questioning. "Jasmine will be running the Grove for us. At least until next summer, when my sister Whitney will join her."

"What on-the-job experience does she have?" Mr. Spencer asked.

"She's overseen the construction so far. She's worked very closely with our contractor here, Mr. Conner."

Jackson gave Charles Spencer a light smile.

"It's true, she is a novice," said Alyson. "We all are. Which is why we were hoping for much more than just capital for this venture—we were hoping for your expertise."

"We certainly have been in this business for a long time, and we have a wealth of knowledge. Should we decide to invest in the Grove, we will provide as much assistance to you as possible," said Charles Spencer. "Darren runs our Nassau property and manages a few others in the States—"

Darren interrupted his father. "And I would be happy to work closely with Jasmine to bring her up to speed on a few things—recruiting and monitoring staff, promoting and marketing, dealing with contractors and suppliers."

His sly grin told me that he was interested in offering more than training.

I shot a glance over at Jackson. He looked as if he was doing everything in his power not to reach over the table and choke the life out of him. Instead he cleared his throat and kept his poker face intact.

Alyson interjected, "I would think that Darren would be too busy to offer one-on-one services like that to Jasmine. Perhaps it might be more appropriate to pair her with one of your female managers. Or even your daughter. Isn't she in the business as well, Mr. Spencer?"

"Yes, she is. Brittany manages our Cat Island property," said Charles.

"Brittany's still on a learning track herself. I, however, have been doing this since college," said Darren. "I can certainly bring more to the table than my younger sister."

"I remember when you were in college, Darren," Alyson said with a veiled edge to her voice. The two of them had an ongoing dislike for each other. "You and Jasmine were so in love. Well, at least Jasmine was. She was convinced that you were her knight in shining armor, and that the two of you were going to marry after graduation. Jasmine was always a bit naive when it came to men."

I didn't quite understand how this conversation was relevant to anything. But this wasn't the appropriate time for her or Darren's antagonism. If she was trying to sabotage the Spencers' investment, she was doing a fantastic job of it.

"I remember that as well," said Charles. He laughed. "Luckily my son found out about her promiscuity beforehand. No offense, Jasmine."

"None taken." Offense was not what I was experiencing. Confusion was. *My promiscuity?*

"Her promiscuity?" Alyson asked what I was thinking. "I don't remember my sister ever being promiscuous a day in her life."

"It was why they broke up," said Mr. Spencer, as if he knew some truth.

"Can we change the subject, please?" asked Darren. "This is neither the place nor time for this discussion."

I couldn't have agreed more.

"I beg to differ," said Alyson. "There's always been a bit of contention between our two families. That's no secret. Wouldn't you say, Mr. Spencer?"

"I would have to agree. We were never on the best of terms, which was why I was very surprised when Edward called this meeting."

"I believe the contention has been mostly due to misinformation," Alyson said. "I think that in order for us to move forward, it might not be a bad idea for us to revisit the past—clear the air. It would make for a much better working relationship, should you decide to invest in the Grove."

"I agree," said Charles Spencer.

"What happened between your son and my sister was a long time ago, but I believe that she has been living with the pain of it ever since. And I think that my sister gets a bad rap all too often," Alyson said.

Was that my sister Alyson defending me? I could hardly believe my ears.

Alyson continued, "Darren, I read about your elaborate wedding in the Eleutheran newspaper. It took place in Nassau two summers ago, at the Atlantis."

"Cost me a pretty penny," Mr. Spencer interjected.

"I'll bet it did. It looked expensive," said Alyson. "What was your wife's name again?"

Darren's demeanor changed. He sank down into his seat a bit and cleared his throat. "Elizabeth."

"Oh yes, that's right. Elizabeth," said Alyson. "I think the article said that the two of you attended college together."

"Yes, we did."

"You dated her in college while my sister was at Spelman, right?" Alyson asked the question but didn't really expect a response. "I remember Jasmine being pretty torn up when she caught the two of you in your dorm together, in a very compromising position. Weren't they in bed together, Jasmine?"

I nodded, but did not speak a word.

"Is that true, son?" Mr. Spencer asked Darren. "I thought it was you who caught Jasmine in her dorm with another fellow."

Darren hung his head.

"Do you and Elizabeth have children, Darren?" asked Alyson.

"Yes, we have two children."

"That's lovely. It's hard to believe that you, Darren Spencer, are all grown up and married—with two children," said Alyson.

Charles Spencer interjected, "Unfortunately, there's been a little trouble in the waters. Elizabeth and the children have moved home with her parents for a spell. Just until she and Darren can sort things out."

"Sorry to hear that. Separation and divorce can be so difficult…and expensive, too. I mean the alimony and child support could really take a toll on a family's wealth. I remember when Edward and his wife divorced. She didn't spare him any grief—or finance, for that matter. It was a good thing we didn't have the Grove at that time. She would've been entitled to a portion of his inheritance, for God's sake," said Alyson. "That would've caused a hardship on our family."

"That is true," Mr. Spencer agreed.

"I would think that it would be extremely difficult for Darren to sort things out with his wife while working so closely here at the Grove with my beautiful sister, his ex-girlfriend."

"You've made your point," Darren said.

Alyson spoke directly to Charles Spencer. "So, sir, if you decide to invest in the Grove—which I hope that you will—I would suggest sending your daughter Brittany to provide that on-the-job training to Jasmine."

"You're very discerning, Alyson. And you're absolutely right," Mr. Spencer agreed. "And thank you for clearing the air."

"My pleasure."

"And, Jasmine, I apologize for misjudging you," Mr. Spencer said and then glared at Darren. "I was obviously given misinformation. Isn't that right, son?"

Darren nodded.

"Please forgive us," said Mr. Spencer.

"I accept your apology, sir. Thank you," I said.

Edward and I visibly exhaled when that conversation was over, and Jackson relaxed a bit. I wasn't sure what Alyson's motives had been. I didn't know if she was protecting me, the Grove or Jackson, but I was grateful for the reprieve. Although Darren had been the love of my life once, and he was still a very gorgeous man, he hadn't been forthcoming with his father or me.

"Now, we should get down to business," said Edward.

"I've gone over your business plan," Mr. Spencer said

and I cringed. I wasn't sure where he was headed, but I braced myself for the worst. However, his next words put me somewhat at ease. "The business plan clearly demonstrates a road map for the Grove's success, and it gives us a realistic forecast for reaping a return on our capital. That is our main concern here."

Edward began his sales pitch. "This is not a unique business in Eleuthera. As you both know, the Bahamas is heavily dependent upon tourism. We have many competitors in this market and even on Harbour Island. The problem with many existing hotels and resorts is that they have a vacationist mentality. The Grove will offer more of a home-away-from-home atmosphere and give the tourist a local, native feel."

Alyson picked up the pitch. "Our target client will be the traveler who wants to feel like an islander, and who veers off the beaten path."

Mr. Spencer nodded. "Your business plan demonstrated that very well."

We spent the afternoon outlining the highlights of our business and negotiating investment terms. It was exhausting, but the reward came when Mr. Spencer announced that he would recommend the Grove as a positive investment to his partners.

"We look forward to hearing from you soon," Alyson said to Mr. Spencer.

We all shook hands.

"I appreciated your honesty at the beginning of the conversation, Alyson. Although there was some contention between the two families, we've always believed the Talbots to be a respectable family," said Mr. Spencer. "We think this will be a wonderful partnership, right, son?"

Darren peered at his father. "I think it's a bit premature to say."

"Of course, I will need to speak with our other principals," said Mr. Spencer, "one being my son here."

"Of course," said Edward.

"But I'm positive that they will all go with my recommendation." Mr. Spencer shook Edward's hand. "We'll be in touch."

After the Spencers left, I rushed to the kitchen and searched the cabinets for the bottle of champagne that I had nestled there. I grabbed four glasses and poured champagne into each one. "Let's toast."

"To the Grove!" said Edward as he held his glass in the air.

"To the Grove!" we all exclaimed in unison.

"We pulled it off," said Edward.

"Thanks to Jasmine's business plan," said Jackson.

"Nope. Thanks to Alyson," I said. "Thank you for setting the record straight about me and Darren."

"I didn't do it for you. I did it for the Grove."

"Still, I thank you," I told her. "And how did you know all that stuff about Elizabeth and me finding the two of them together in his college dorm?"

"It wasn't hard to put it together."

"Why haven't you ever shared this with me? That you knew all along."

"Why didn't you share with me that you were hurt by that creep?"

"I didn't think you cared."

"I don't." Alyson smirked. "Okay, maybe I care a little. You're still my sister."

It was the nicest thing she'd said to me in years, and it warmed my heart. I smiled.

"And don't think I don't know about you and Jackson Conner over there," Alyson said.

"What?" Jackson asked innocently.

"Oh, don't play dumb with me. The two of you have been running around this island together for weeks, thinking that you've been inconspicuous. News flash, you haven't been."

"What are you talking about, Alyson?" Edward asked.

"Oh, Edward. Wake up. They're in love. It's so obvious. Didn't you see how uncomfortable Jackson was when Darren was coming on to Jasmine? He wanted to rearrange his face." Alyson laughed. "I had to step in and save the poor man."

"Thank you, I guess," said Jackson.

"Why didn't I know that the two of you were in love?" asked Edward.

"I wanted to tell you, bro. I just didn't know how," said Jackson. "I didn't want you to think that my relationship with Jasmine would affect my ability to do the work at the Grove."

"Well, the work at the Grove is impeccable. So it's obvious there's no conflict," Edward said. "Besides, I thought the two of you hated each other."

"We did at first," I told him. "But then something happened along the way."

"You have to take care of my sister," Edward threatened. "Because if you don't…I don't know what I would do to you."

"You don't have to worry about that," said Jackson. "I'm completely devoted to Jasmine."

"Blah, blah, blah. All of this is making me want to gag," said Alyson. "Can we go now? I've got a plane to catch. I need to get back to Miami tonight. I have a closing in the morning."

"Jackson and I will be in Miami this weekend," I told Alyson. "Maybe you and I can have lunch or something while I'm there."

"We'll see," said Alyson. "There's a café in Little Havana that I frequent. They've got the best garlic chicken and the best café Cubano. Maybe we can go there, if you have time. But don't do anything special on my account."

"It's a date. I'll see you Saturday."

"Fine." She headed toward the door and opened it wide, then glared at Edward.

"I need to absorb all of this," Edward said. "I'll let you know how I feel about it later."

I kissed my brother's cheek. "He's a good man, Edward."

"I know he's a good man. We've been friends for a long time. I just don't know how I feel about him doing…you know…things with my little sister. Now, that's disturbing."

"Let's go." Alyson pulled Edward out the door.

She gave me a wink and a half smile as she exited. It almost felt as though I had my sister back.

Chapter 20

Jasmine

We drove the stretch of US-1 toward Miami, with the windows down and hip-hop music blaring on the stereo. Devante stretched his long legs across the backseat of our rental car. An iPod in his hand and earbuds in his ears, he bounced his head up and down. Jackson looked at him in the rearview mirror and mentioned to me how much he'd grown since the last time he'd seen him. Jackson had unofficially been Devante's mentor since he was twelve years old. Now at seventeen, he was just as tall as Jackson.

I hadn't been told the whole story about our trip. I knew that we were flying into Key West and that we had tickets to a Miami Heat game. Jackson had also mentioned something about a teenage boy, nachos and repaying a debt to the boy's mother. Eventually, I managed to piece all the details together. In exchange for Tracy locating my laptop, Jackson had promised to spend some quality time with her teenage son. Devante's grades were slipping and his mother was concerned that he was falling in with the wrong crowd. She wanted Jackson to have a conversation with him and get him back on the right track. It warmed my heart to know that Jackson was willing to be the male figure that the teen needed. It was a testament to the type of man he was, and it made him much more attractive.

It had to be hard for Tracy to raise a young man on her own. I couldn't imagine our mother raising us alone. Especially the boys, who needed the voice and hand of my father. He'd taught them things that my mother would never have been able to instill. All of my brothers had grown up to be strong, educated and upstanding men. And it was because of my father. Jackson also had a strong man in his life. Although he'd recently changed his opinion of the man who'd raised him, his stepfather still had been there. He'd given him the tools that he needed to navigate through life. And although I thought that Jackson should've been more grateful to John Conner for giving him what some young men never receive in a lifetime, I was happy that he realized the importance of giving that same nurturing to Devante.

I turned around in my seat, and touched Devante's knee and gave him a smile. He removed his earbuds.

"Ever been to a professional basketball game before?" I asked him.

"Never!" he exclaimed.

"Me either. I can't wait," I told him. "Do you play sports?"

"Basketball and football. I'm on both teams at school."

"Are you any good?"

"I start."

"He's very talented," Jackson said. "His mother keeps me up on all his stats. I think football is more his game, though."

"You mind if I check out one of your games some-time?" I asked.

Devante shrugged. "Okay."

"Cool. Maybe you can send me your schedule, then." I jotted down my email address on a piece of paper and handed it to Devante.

He looked at it and stuffed it into the pocket of his jeans, and then waited a few moments to see if I was done talking, anxious to stick the earbuds back into his ears. To his surprise, I wasn't done and ended up capturing his ear throughout the entire three-hour drive. We talked about everything from sports to music to girls. Through our conversation I gathered that there was one particular girl that held his interest—Ashley. But he was afraid to talk to her. I gave him a few pointers on how to approach her, and he listened intently. I was certain that she'd be his girlfriend by the end of the next week.

Before we reached Miami, it was clear that Devante had developed a small crush on me. His body language had changed toward me and he was now asking me questions.

"So you grew up in the Bahamas your whole life?"

"My whole life," I told him. "Maybe you can come over sometime, and I'll show you around. Lots of pretty young girls over there. Of course, you'll be in a relationship with Ashley soon, so you probably won't really care about other girls."

"Do they look like you?" Devante grinned from ear to ear. Colorful braces adorned his teeth.

"Some of them do, I suppose."

"They're beautiful, but not quite as beautiful as my girl." Jackson gave Devante a glance in the rearview mirror.

"Are you two going to get married?" Devante asked.

I shrugged and Jackson responded.

"Someday, maybe?" Jackson looked at me as if he expected me to respond. "Marriage is a huge step, but not totally out of the question…for us…maybe…"

"We hadn't really thought…talked about it," I said.

"It would be kind of hard, considering she lives in the Bahamas and I live in Key West," Jackson added.

"Exactly. Not to mention, after he finishes work on the Grove, he'll go back home to Florida and I'll be some long-lost memory."

Jackson gave me a sideways look. "What she means is that she'll probably totally forget about me."

We'd gotten caught up in our own awareness of our relationship, and totally forgot about Devante's initial question.

"I just wanted to know if I could come to the wedding," Devante interjected.

It was apparent that a future conversation needed to take place between Jackson and me.

"You'll be one of the first people to receive an invitation, if we ever decide to get married," said Jackson. "And I'm not saying that we will, but…"

"If you don't marry her, I sure will." Devante laughed.

"Very funny!" Jackson laughed, too. "You'll never be old enough to marry her. I think you'd better stick with Ashley."

The three of us laughed and talked until we finally pulled up in front of the American Airlines Arena. We enjoyed an action-packed game, and I cheered every time the Heat scored a basket and cursed when the other team did. By the fourth quarter, we were all standing and whistling with each play.

It was bumper-to-bumper traffic as we left the arena's parking lot and made our way toward South Beach. We managed to snag a parking space and strolled the board-walk under the moonlight. People zoomed by on a set of Rollerblades, and Devante snapped photos of beautiful women sporting skimpy bikinis. We peeked inside ex-pensive boutiques and window-shopped and then enjoyed deep-dish pizza and cannolis at a local restaurant. At the end of the night, we stopped at Starbucks for lattes before turning in at our downtown hotel.

In our two-bedroom suite, Jackson and I took separate rooms while Devante slept on the sofa sleeper in the living area. I lay awake in my empty bed, stared at the ceiling for a while and then toyed with my phone for a bit. I checked email and my newsfeed on Facebook. I flipped the televi-sion on and channel-surfed, but unable to find anything that kept my interest, I flipped the television off and lay awake in the dark until my eyelids finally grew heavy.

Sometime in the middle of the night, I felt Jackson's body slide into bed next to mine. He wrapped his arms around me tightly and kissed my eyelids until I opened them.

"What are you doing in here?" I asked.

"Couldn't sleep," he whispered. "Needed to be near you."

"What if Devante wakes up?"

"He won't."

His lips kissed mine, and his tongue danced inside my mouth. His hand traveled to my breasts, squeezed them gently and then danced across my belly. I trembled from the coldness of his touch. When his fingertips caressed the insides of my thighs, my heart thumped rapidly. My breathing changed and my stomach trembled. His fingers found the wetness between my thighs and I moaned loudly.

"Shhh," he whispered.

I giggled as he continued to explore the sensitive parts of my body with his lips and fingertips.

"I love you, Jackson," I whispered. It was the first time I'd proclaimed my love to him, although I'd known about it for some time. I knew the first time we'd made love that I needed him in my life.

His lips hungrily engulfed mine, and he aggressively pulled my legs apart and swiftly removed my panties. He planted a trail of kisses from my lips to my neck, moved his way down to my breasts and laved my firm nipples. Soon I felt soft kisses on my stomach and a tongue circling my navel. He lingered near my abdomen before surprising my inner thighs with his gentle exploration. By the time his tongue reached my tender place, I was grasping the bed's headboard. My bare toes curled as I attempted to regain control. It seemed I always lost control when I was with Jackson. He caused my body to experience things it had never felt before and always left me longing for more.

Jackson removed his pajama bottoms, and before I could think twice, he'd already entered me. His breath was warm against my ear. We moved together in a perfect rhythm, and I dug my fingernails into his back. His lips found mine again and we kissed vivaciously until we both discovered our peak. I was sure I'd found the true meaning of euphoria as Jackson's heavy body collapsed on top of mine. Exhausted, he slid onto his back and both of us lay there silently for a few moments.

Soon I felt his strong arms wrap themselves around my waist from behind and squeeze tightly.

"You drive me crazy," he whispered in my ear. "I can't even describe what I feel when we're together."

"It's called testosterone," I teased.

"It's called captivation," he said. "I'm enamored by you, Jasmine Talbot."

"And I, you."

"You've come in and rearranged my entire life. Got me doing things that I'd almost forgotten how to do, like live. It's been a long time since I've taken time from my busy schedule and done anything fun," he said. "You have me enjoying life."

"Life is short, Jackson. If you don't enjoy it, you'll miss it."

"I only want to enjoy it with you."

"I don't see that happening beyond the Grove," I said. "Once the project is complete, you'll go back to your home in Key West."

"Will you visit me?"

"Of course," I told him. "We can try commuting back and forth between Florida and the Bahamas for a while, but we both know that long-distance relationships never work. Eventually, you'll go back to your workaholic lifestyle and I'll be inundated with work at the Grove."

"And we'll lose all of this?"

"I honestly don't see any other way," I told him. "I've made up my mind to just enjoy what we have right now. I don't want to think about what happens after the Grove. Don't want to get my hopes up, only to be disappointed by a man again."

"I understand," he said.

They were hard words, but I needed to speak them. Love had been unexpected and I wasn't willing to allow myself to get off track again in my life. I was committed to the Grove, and that was all.

"I'd rather we live for right now and enjoy this for as long as we can," I whispered.

"Me too." He kissed my neck and then stood up, and I couldn't help but revel in his nakedness. But then he picked up his clothes and began to dress.

"Where you going?"

"Back to my room before Devante wakes up."

"Okay," I whispered.

He was gone too quickly, and left me with too many questions racing through my head.

I checked the address of the tall, glass-and-steel upscale structure that was Alyson's building. I said goodbye to Jackson and Devante, who had plans to shoot hoops at the local community center for the day, and I went through the lobby and up the elevator to the door of her condo. She answered wearing a gray business suit and holding a cell phone. Fully engaged in her conversation, she gestured me in and I made my way into the living room. It was the first time I'd visited my sister's home, and I looked around—really scrutinized the place. With colorless art on the walls and her sensible furniture, her home was just as I'd imagined it would be— quintessential Alyson.

I perused the books on her bookshelf—many of which were self-help or real estate. I noticed that she had a particular fixation for books about leadership and power. There weren't any family photographs on the wall or shelves, just a few vases and expensive-looking artifacts. The kitchen was spotless, with granite counters that sparkled from the sunlight and stainless-steel appliances. The wooden dining room table held a huge basket filled with fresh fruit—bananas, oranges and mangoes. Her hardwoods were impeccable. I stepped over to the picture window and looked down at the Miami River—a breathtaking view. It was the liveliest part of the home, and I could've stood there forever and just taken it in. Instead, I took a seat on the leather sectional, grabbed the remote control and flipped on the television. Alyson continued to chat on the phone, while I flipped through the channels.

"Sorry about that, Jasmine," she said once she was done.

"Let me slip into something a little more comfortable before we go. Make yourself at home."

I did just that. Slipping my embellished sandals from my feet and curling them underneath my bottom, I forced myself to relax. After all, it was my sister's home. As different as we both were, the same blood that ran through my veins ran through hers. She was the same sister I'd grown up with in our home on Governor's Harbour. I would find my way into her life if it killed me.

"Okay, let's go." She entered the room wearing a casual pantsuit, which was way more conservative than the blue jeans I'd chosen for the day and the sexy, fuchsia-colored knit sweater that hung below the shoulder line.

"I'm not underdressed, am I?"

She scrutinized my outfit. "It'll do."

We made our way into the parking garage and hopped into Alyson's pewter-colored convertible BMW. My body sank down into the black leather seats as she let the top down and we pulled out of the garage and onto a busy thoroughfare. She quickly maneuvered through traffic toward Little Havana, an area in the center of the Miami Cuban community. We cruised past Calle Ocho, the famous street, and the Walk of Fame, down the Cuban Memorial Boulevard and the Tower Theater. My hair blew in the wind.

Alyson parked the car at a meter on the street and paid with her credit card. We stepped out and strolled past the mom-and-pop shops that lined the streets—boutiques, cigar shops and Cuban restaurants. We walked past the famous Domino Park, where several older gentlemen gathered and competed in games of dominoes. My mouth watered for a Cuban sandwich garnished with Swiss cheese, mustard and pickles on a baguette—the ones they served at just about every family-owned eatery along the strip, but Alyson had another place in mind.

"This is my favorite restaurant," she said as we stepped inside the café and were greeted by soft Spanish music.

A Cuban hostess led us to the small table near a window. She mumbled something in broken English before handing us a menu. The smell of strong spices filled the room—reminiscent of the spices we used in Bahamian cooking. It was apparent why Alyson loved the place so much.

"It feels like home," I said.

"That's what I like about it." She smiled. "That and the garlic chicken, pastelitos and Cuban coffee."

"What are pastelitos?"

"It's a pastry with guava and cheese. We'll have it for dessert," explained Alyson.

"May I take your drink order, ladies?" A beautiful Cuban server appeared at our table.

"I'll have a mojito," said Alyson, "and one for my sister."

"Since when do you drink in the middle of the day?" I asked.

"I have an occasional nip," she said, "during special times."

I smiled inside. She considered this a special time.

"Order my lunch for me, too," I said. I wanted to experience my sister's special place through her eyes.

"Okay, let's see." She looked over the menu. "We'll start with some croquetas and sweet plantains. You order the Cuban sandwich. I know that's your style."

"You know me too well."

"And I'll order the garlic chicken. That way we can share, and we both get a taste of each other's food."

"Sounds good."

After placing our order with the server, I gazed out the window and watched as people strolled past. I was afraid that our dinner conversation would be strained, as my sister and I knew very little about each other and had even less to talk about. Her phone rang and she took the call, but wrapped it up quickly. Then she shut the ringer off and stuck the phone into her purse.

"So tell me about Jackson," she said. "How did the two of you end up…you know, hooking up?"

I was taken aback by her question. She jumped right in there and asked what she wanted to know. So typical of her.

"I don't know. It just happened. One day we were fighting and the next he was kissing me."

"He's very handsome. Is he a worthy lover?" she asked.

I laughed. The question seemed strange coming from my sister, who quite possibly hadn't had a worthy lover in some time.

"Yes, he is." I blushed and answered honestly.

"I know you think I'm a stick in the mud, but I'm not. I might not live as interesting a life as you, but I'm not a prude."

I almost asked, *"You're not?"* Instead I lied and said, "I didn't think you were a prude."

"I've had my share of handsome, worthy men. Just no one that I wanted to spend any considerable amount of time with," she said. "I want a man just like my daddy and they just aren't out there anymore. Our dad is one of a kind."

"I agree. I've always wanted a man like Daddy, too. I think Jackson is very much like our father. He's gentle and kind, hardworking, a man's man," I said. "I love him."

"Don't be fooled by love, Jasmine. Love is an illusion," said Alyson. "Besides, it could never work between you two. You live worlds apart. When he's done with the Grove, he'll return home to Key West. And then what? You planning to move to Key West or are you planning to date him long-distance?"

"We're just going to enjoy what we have now and worry about later…later."

"Smart girl. Don't be fooled into thinking that this can last long-term," said Alyson. "I never let any man get too close. It's too risky to put my heart out there. Besides, men are intimidated by my wealth and independence. I'll die alone."

That was a sad thought—that my sister might never find someone to spend the rest of her life with. She would cause her own demise and miss out on love because she was too rigid.

When our drinks arrived, I took a sip.

"Haven't you met anyone that you loved even a little bit?"

"Just one man. Jimmy Franklin. Well, he wasn't a man at the time. He was a boy," she said matter-of-factly. "But we both know how that ended."

"I'm very sorry about Jimmy Franklin," I told her.

I was afraid that topic might come up. It was the one conversation that I dreaded having with my sister. I sighed and took a long sip of my drink. I needed it if we were going to tread the *Jimmy Franklin* waters.

"I've always thought that you wanted him, and I hated you for so long because of it." She took a long sip of her mojito.

"I wanted him?" I took another swallow of my drink and decided now was the time for honesty. Maybe it was the mojito talking, but I said, "I hated him. Jimmy made advances toward me when you weren't around. My rejection only encouraged him more. Ultimately he tried to rape me."

Alyson looked positively shocked. "What? He tried to rape you?"

"Yes."

"Tell me what happened," she said.

I wanted to forget the details of Jimmy Franklin's attempted rape. Wanted to wipe the thought of it from my mind forever.

"What do you mean?"

"Tell me how it happened. I want all the details."

I sighed. Was she serious?

"I need to put this behind me," she said, "please."

I finished my drink and then signaled for the server to bring me another. "Um, I was on my way home from school one day. I had to stay late because I had a detention. You'd already gone home early, and Edward had basketball practice. Whitney, who I usually walked home with, had stayed home that day. So I had no choice but to walk home alone. He was teasing me about my hair."

"I cut it," Alyson remembered. "You had a piece of gum stuck in your hair, and I tried cutting it out. Left you looking crazy."

"Yes, exactly. I was embarrassed to go to school like that, but I went anyway. Jimmy followed me home, teasing me about my hair the whole way. And I just ignored him. That only made him angry, and then he grabbed me. Tried to kiss me and I pushed him away."

"And?" She hung on my every word.

"And then he got rough with me." I couldn't look at her anymore as I continued. "He pinned me against that old banyan tree and forced my underwear to the ground. I kneed him in the groin and took off running."

"Bastard!" Her response startled me.

"When I got home, I told Daddy what happened. Next thing I knew, he was gone and not too soon."

When I looked up, Alyson had tears in her eyes. I didn't know how to comfort her.

"I'm sorry that it happened, Alyson. I didn't mean to have the love of your life sent away, but…"

"I'm not crying for him," she said. "I'm crying for you. I'm sorry that it happened to you. I didn't know."

"I asked Daddy not to tell you or the others. I was too embarrassed."

"All this time…" She wiped tears away with her cloth napkin. "All these years we lost."

"You didn't know."

"I'm sorry, Jasmine."

I went over to my sister, knelt down beside her and held her. I didn't care that every eye in the restaurant was on us. We needed that moment.

"I need you, Alyson. I need my sister. I'm so alone in this world."

"I'm here. You never have to feel alone again."

I rested my head on my sister's shoulder and we cried and rocked for a few more moments before I went back to my seat. I didn't want us to be escorted from the premises. We both laughed a deep, hearty, alcohol-filled laugh, embarrassed for having caused a scene in Alyson's favorite place.

After our food arrived, we ate off each other's plates and enjoyed every delightful morsel together. We each had three more mojitos and then tried to sober up with an after-dinner café con leche—a shot of Cuban coffee with milk.

We sat in Alyson's favorite café for what seemed like a lifetime, talking and laughing and catching up on old times, discussing how we'd missed out on so much of each other's lives. The last real conversation we'd had was during our adolescence. Beyond that, I didn't know my sister and she didn't know me. Somehow, we'd gotten stuck in time, both too stubborn to make amends. But that had all changed now.

Once we were sober, Alyson maneuvered her BMW back toward her downtown condo. Once there, it wasn't long before we both fell asleep on her leather sectional—

she at one end and me at the other. The doorbell jarred us from our slumber. Alyson looked as if she'd been in a street fight as she answered the door.

Jackson cautiously stepped inside.

"Are y'all okay?" he asked. Devante stood close behind.

I undoubtedly looked as if I'd been in that same street fight.

"We're fine," Alyson answered.

"Couldn't be better," I responded.

"Okay," he said. "Are you ready to go? I wanna get on the road before nightfall."

"Of course." I stood. "Just let me run to the bathroom first and freshen up. Then we can go."

"Linen is in the hall closet," said Alyson.

I stopped in the hallway, grabbed a washcloth. In the small powder room, I stared at my reflection in the mirror. My eyeliner and eye shadow were smeared across my face. With warm water, I washed my face, refreshed my makeup and combed my hair. I smiled at the woman who smiled back at me in the mirror. Today had been a good day.

I gave my sister the longest hug goodbye. Didn't want to let go.

"I love you, Jazzy," she said. She rarely ever used my family nickname. In fact, she always used my birth name and said it with such contempt. But today, I was *Jazzy*.

"Ditto," I said.

"Text me when you get to Key West."

"I promise."

As Jackson merged onto US-1, he looked over at me with those ravishing eyes.

"I'm not even going to ask what just went on back there," he said.

"Just know that it was something very, very wonderful." I smiled.

It was the last thing I said before resting my head back and sleeping the entire way to Key West. I didn't even remember dropping Devante off at home. I missed telling him goodbye.

Chapter 21

Jackson

"Do you play bid whist, Jasmine?" my mother asked, sipping on a vodka tonic.

"Are you supposed to be drinking, Mother?" I intercepted her question to Jasmine.

It hadn't been long since her surgery and I was concerned that she'd gone back to sipping alcohol too soon.

"I'm just having a little taste, Jax. Nothing more. I'm enjoying my night and my family," my mother said. "Come, Jasmine. Let me see you."

Jasmine did as my mother asked and walked over to the side of the card table where she sat. She laid her cards facedown on the table and grabbed both of Jasmine's hands.

"She's pretty, Jax." She patted the empty chair that rested against the wall. "Here, sit next to me, honey. You'll be my good-luck charm."

Jasmine took the seat next to my mother. My brother

Drew sat across the table from Mother. He was her card partner. My brother Sean and John Conner sat in the opposite two chairs. I gave Jasmine a look of apology, which she dismissed. She seemed comfortable there, as Mother began to explain the game of bid whist to her.

I had been nervous about taking Jasmine to Key West to meet my family, and particularly my mother. My family could be judgmental and opinionated. Sometimes even embarrassing. My mother had a special sense about people. She could see right through them. She'd know what their intentions were long before anyone else knew. And she wasn't afraid to call them out. Mother could give me a look from across the room and I'd know exactly what she was thinking. So far, though, I hadn't seen that look. Instead she gave me a smile of approval as she and Jasmine became cozier by the minute.

Saturday nights at the Conner household were never boring. There was always card playing, music, good food and laughter. Sometimes it would be just family, sometimes other relatives and friends, but there was always something going on. There would always be a keg of beer in the kitchen and John Conner was usually out back nursing the barbecue smoker. It was during those times that he bonded with his sons, over the barbecue grill. He taught us some of our greatest lessons while slapping sauce onto a slab of ribs.

Al Green crooned on Mother's old stereo. On that old stereo, you might hear the blues, gospel, New Orleans jazz and even classical music. Sometimes my mother would sing and my brothers and I would join her. We had all inherited her gift of song. The music could be heard throughout the two-story traditional home in Old Town. After Katrina, I had assisted Jett Prim in the renovation of the property. We'd installed Brazilian cherry floors and custom kitchen cabinets. We'd also built a deck that surrounded the home—it was an anniversary gift to them. The home was gorgeous and a very comfortable place to have grown up in.

Drew was the only one to return home after college. Eli had gotten married and made his home in New York. Sean returned to Florida and landed a job at an engineering firm in West Palm Beach. Although he'd purchased a waterfront property near his office, he still commuted to Key West just about every weekend. My home was not far from my parents'. However, they rarely saw me because I was always working and often traveling. And after the whole ordeal of discovering that John Conner wasn't my biological father, my presence here was almost nonexistent. In fact, this was the first time I'd stepped foot into the Conner household since then.

Nothing had changed much, besides the fact that my mother rearranged the furniture on a regular basis. She was never satisfied with things, which I guessed was part of the reason why she'd stepped out on John Conner those many years ago. Always looking for something better. I assumed she'd finally learned that the grass wasn't always greener on the other side.

I poured myself a beer and one for Jasmine, who was now seated across from my mother at the table. She had become Mother's bid-whist partner, and she seemed to be handling her own in a game that she'd learned only less than an hour before. She'd even followed my mother's lead and commenced to talking trash to the other team. Soon, the four of them seemed like old friends.

"She's sexy, Jax," said Drew after he'd been dismissed from the card table. With a sly grin on his face and his hand on his chin, he asked, "You serious about her?"

"Very," I said. I knew exactly where he was going with that question.

Drew loved women—of all shapes, sizes and colors.

"Seems Mother likes her," he said.

"It does seem that way, doesn't it? Jasmine's a very likable woman."

At that moment, she caught my eye from across the room and I gave her a kiss in the air. She winked.

"Mother never liked anybody I brought home." Drew took a sip of his beer. It seemed he'd had one too many by then. "But then, you always were her favorite. You could bring King Kong home and she wouldn't care."

"That's not true. She never liked anyone I brought home before now."

"Well, now that I think about it, I guess you're right," he laughed, "because she couldn't stand that girl Denise."

He laughed but that was a sore spot for me. I'd wanted her to like Denise so badly, just to make my life easier. I was never going to have a future with Denise—that was apparent, but I needed some peace while the relationship lasted. And my mother had refused to give me that.

"Yeah, she hated Denise, didn't she?"

"Mother is a hard woman."

"She just loves her boys and only wants what's best for us."

"I'm glad to see you back here, Jackson. Mother and Dad missed you something crazy. Daddy has nothing but mad love for you. I mean, I don't know what this guy in New Orleans is like, but he'll never love you like my father does. And that's a fact, Jack." He started to walk away. "Now let me go show these folks how to play some cards."

He stood next to John Conner at the card table and motioned for him to relinquish his seat.

"Come on, Jax, and play some cards!" said Mother.

"I'm fine, Mom. I'm going to step outside on the deck and have a word with John," I told her. She smiled. It was a conversation that she'd encouraged for so long, and I was finally prepared to have it. It was one of the reasons I'd come home. I had a few things I needed to say. "Can you step out here with me?" I asked him.

"Of course." He poured himself another beer and then followed me outside to the deck that I'd helped build.

I took a seat in one of the easy chairs, crossed my legs wide. John took a seat across from me.

"What's on your mind, son?"

This time when he called me son, it didn't anger me or make me defensive.

"I went to see that Patrick Wells dude," I told him.

"Oh yeah?" he asked, "and how did that go?" John Conner never got excited about anything. He was a calm man.

"He pretty much rejected me and threw me out of his office. I guess I got what I deserved for popping up on him like that."

"You didn't deserve to be lied to and kept in the dark," he said. "And I'm sorry for being a participant in that. You had a right to know, Jackson."

"Yeah, I did. But I'm past that now," I told him. "I brought you out here because I want you to know that I appreciate your being my father for all these years. Teaching me everything that I know, encouraging me when I was down, showing me the value of a good education. Not only did you teach me how to be a man, you demonstrated it for me every single day. And I'm grateful."

John Conner became choked up. He turned his head away from me, looked out into the yard at the palm trees swaying in the wind as tears crept down his cheeks. When he'd gathered himself, he turned back to me. "I'd do it all again. You're my son."

"Why do you think my biological father rejected me?"

"Who knows, Jackson? Some men are cowards. They're

only men when others are watching or when they're in the public eye. Real men do what they have to do no matter who's watching. And they own up to their mistakes. And they right their wrongs," said John Conner. "But you can't worry about the next man, Jackson…"

It was a phrase that I'd heard often. It was instilled in us as boys. *You can't worry about the next man.*

"You can only do what you know is right," I said, completing the sentence.

"Exactly." He smiled, pride covering his face. "You've done your part, son. Now he must do his, whatever that is."

"I love you, Dad," I told him and meant it. All four words.

As he stood and reached for my hand, I stood and gave my father a hug.

"I love you, too, son," he said.

"Where do we go from here?" I asked.

"We pick right back up where we left off. We don't miss a beat. We move forward like this never happened."

Tears filled my eyes as I listened to his words. When he let me go, I glanced to my left. My mother and Jasmine stood in the glass doorway, their arms interlocked. They both smiled at us.

All was well in the Conner household again.

Jasmine and I drove the short distance to my renovated bungalow. I hadn't been home in some time, and I hoped that I'd left the place in decent condition. It was stuffy inside, so I immediately opened a window to allow fresh air inside and turned on the ceiling fan.

"Make yourself at home," I told Jasmine. "The bathroom is around the corner there if you need to freshen up or take a shower."

"This is cute, Jackson. It's so you."

"It's a small place, but it's mine. I like it."

She dropped her shoes at the door and then took the liberty of looking around, popping her head into every room. "Where do you hang out?"

"Right here, in the living room in front of the television set. My laptop in hand."

"That's your favorite seat?" she asked about my leather easy chair.

"How'd you guess?"

"I just knew." She plopped down in my chair and reclined. "It's by the window so you can be nosy."

"I'm not nosy," I told her.

"There's a lot going on out there, Jackson," she said, peeking through my blinds. "I would be nosy if I lived here."

"Yeah, my neighbors are pretty colorful. But when I'm here, I just ignore them as much as I can."

"I love your mother," she said. "She's so funny."

"And she loves you. But I'm not surprised. You're easy to love."

"Your family is great. Your stepdad is sweet."

"My dad." I smiled. "That's my dad."

"I'm so proud of you for making amends with him. He's a good man and so are you." She curled up in my chair, making it seem less manly.

"He raised me, so I guess it would make sense that we're both good men."

"I guess it would." She hopped up. "I'm going to shower."

"Mind if I join you?"

"Not at all."

With bare feet, she padded into the kitchen and started opening cabinets and drawers—in search of something. I wasn't sure what until she walked back into the living room, carrying several candles of all shapes and sizes. She found a book of matches and lit every candle, placed them all around the house. I didn't even know I had that many candles. I'd used them only for light when I lost power, but as she lit them and turned on the stereo, I knew her intention was far different.

"Which one is your favorite?" she asked, looking through my CDs.

I walked over and pulled out a Musiq Soulchild CD. It was appropriate for the mood that Jasmine was trying to set. I popped it into my state-of-the-art system and as the music permeated the room Jasmine and I began to slow-dance.

I pulled my T-shirt over my head, slipped out of my shoes, removed my pants, socks, and stripped down to my boxers. She mimicked me and in no time she stood in my living room wearing nothing more than a lacy bra and matching panties. She teased me by loosening the hooks of her bra. Then slowly she took it off, tossed it my way and then rushed into the bathroom. I followed and grabbed her small waist from behind. I turned her around and kissed her lips, slowly removing her panties and then my boxers.

She started the shower and got the water just right. We stepped in together and I stood there, admired Jasmine's glorious body as the water cascaded over her nakedness. I lathered some shower gel in the palm of my hand and spread it over Jasmine's beautiful brown breasts.

"Turn around and I'll wash your back," I told her.

She did as I asked and then I lathered her back. I wrapped my arms tightly around her for a moment and closed my eyes. Thoughts of our conversation the night before had plagued my mind all day. I could barely shoot hoops with Devante earlier, for thinking of it. The thought of losing Jasmine once the Grove was complete was more than disturbing. I wanted to enjoy what we had at the moment, too, but who was I kidding? I needed her in my life long-term.

But I knew that love after the Grove would be next to impossible. The reality was we lived worlds apart. She was committed to the Grove and I was committed to my business. She was comfortable at her home on the islands, and I loved my renovated bungalow in Key West. It was easier for me here. Most of my work was in Florida and my parents lived around the corner. Key West was my home, and Eleuthera was hers. Too many sacrifices would have to be made, and which of us was willing to make them?

"What are you thinking about?" She turned to face me and caressed my chest with her soft hands.

"All the things I'm going to do to your sexy body when we get out of here." I looked into my woman's eyes and knew that I could never let her go.

Maybe we could make the long distance work for us. We owed it to each other to at least try. The Bahamas was a short flight from Florida. We could see each other every weekend, and holidays, too. It could work. It didn't have to be the end of us. I wouldn't let it be.

The flight back to Eleuthera seemed long and exhausting. I held on to Jasmine's hand the whole way. She fell asleep on my shoulder and I gently kissed the top of her head before falling asleep myself. By the time I'd awakened, the plane was on a slow descent. And when the wheels brushed against the runway, I knew we were finally home. At least it was beginning to feel like home for me.

Chapter 22

Jasmine
Three months later

I flipped through a magazine and spotted the advertisement for the Grove. A photo of the gorgeous beachfront property just about leaped from the pages. Thanks to the Spencers' generous investment, we were able to extend our advertising budget beyond its original limit. The Grove was being advertised in world-renowned magazines, local newspapers and those abroad. We even had a television commercial spot being planned for the spring. Our marketing campaign was well under way.

Under Brittany Spencer's watchful eye, I became an expert at the day-to-day run of the house. I had successfully hired a complete staff—a Bahamian chef, a housekeeper for each house, an accountant. I would take reservations and check guests into the property, at least until the task became too overwhelming for me to handle, at which time

I would hire a front desk clerk. My job would be to oversee the staff and ensure that the property ran smoothly.

Meanwhile, my days had been filled with bringing the new staff up to speed, putting the finishing touches on the interior of each house, and also planning the celebration of the Grove's Grand Opening, which was right around the corner. So far, I'd hired a local Caribbean band and the caterers. Christmastime in the Bahamas was festive, and the palm trees out front had been decorated in multicolored lights. Poinsettias and holly adorned the inside of the house. Invitations had been mailed, and RSVPs were slowly trickling in. Hundreds of people would attend the elegant affair, including every one of my siblings. Even Denny would make it home in time.

I'd been so busy I barely had time to spend a single evening gazing at the stars with Jackson. He'd been busy, too, working well into the middle of each night just to meet the Grove's construction deadline. It wasn't long after our trip to Miami and Key West that the Talbot House was completed and work had begun on the third house, Samson Place. A tranquil and serene retreat for lovers, the beachside home had everything desired for a romantic week in the Bahamas—jetted Jacuzzi bathtubs, cozy canopy beds with sheer drapes suspended from the posts to create an intimate scene. Guest packages would include breakfast in bed and complimentary bottles of wine or champagne.

Samson Place would've been the perfect place for Jackson and me to spend our days and nights. Perhaps we should've started construction on this house first. Although we weren't in love in the beginning—in fact, we weren't even in like. But love had certainly developed over time. The theme for the Samson Place would've been a great tribute to the love that we eventually found for each other. However, it was a love that we'd both become uncertain about as the time drew closer for Jackson to return to Key West.

We had managed to stay connected during the busy times, sending text messages to each other several times a day, just to say hi. We made promises of things we'd planned to do to each other by nightfall, only to fall asleep in each other's arms by the time the night actually came, too exhausted to fulfill those promises. But it was nice to simply be held through the night. Just knowing that he was there beside me made me feel safe and gave me great comfort. What would I do without him in the days to come?

I tried to wish the thoughts away, but the truth was I'd grown accustomed to spending every night with Jackson and awakening to his handsome face each morning. I needed him like the air I breathed. Our lives had become too intertwined, and I was so in love with him. We both knew that renovation at the Grove wouldn't last forever. We knew that the day would come when he'd have to return to his home. After all, he was a businessman, and another contracting job awaited him in Fort Lauderdale. And after that, there'd be another. His life was there, not here in Eleuthera, and it was time I faced that truth. It was nice to live in the moment. That way you didn't lose time worrying about tomorrow—you got to enjoy every single smile, laugh, kiss, touch—all the things you might miss if you were busy worrying about things that were out of your control. But the flip side of that is when the moments end, you're left with emptiness and pain.

As much as I had prepared myself for that dreadful day, nothing had prepared me for what I felt now when I saw Jackson's bags resting at the front door of the Clydesdale. Materials and tools had already been packed up and shipped back to the States ahead of him, and many of his employees had returned as well, including Jorge, Diego, Tristan and Lance. I missed our smoke breaks together, even though I never smoked a day in my life. I had thoroughly enjoyed our vivacious conversations. I missed them, but not nearly as much as I would miss the gorgeous copper-colored man with the curly locks, a dazzling smile, boisterous laughter and the ability to make my body feel things that no other man ever could.

He stood at the top of the stairs staring down at me for a few moments. And then he made his way down. "My flight leaves at six," he said.

"This is harder than I thought it would be," I told him.

"For me, too," he said, "but we'll commute for a while, until we tire of it."

"What happens when we *tire* of it, Jackson?" I didn't particularly like his choice of words.

He placed a gentle hand against my face. "I'm sorry, sweetheart. I don't mean to sound so insensitive about it, but I'm a realist and I have to be honest with myself."

"So when you get tired of the commute, does that mean you fall in love with someone else—someone who's more accessible?"

"I can't see loving anyone else but you," he said. "And what about you? You'll be fraternizing with all these rich, successful businessmen who will be frequenting the Grove. What happens when you fall in love with one of them? You'll forget all about poor old Jackson Conner. He was just your little boy toy, a willing participant in your little trysts."

"You don't believe that."

"What am I to believe when the woman I'm hopelessly in love with tells me *let's just live in the moment*?"

"What's the alternative? Do I pack up and move to Key West—abandon my family and the Grove?"

"Of course not," he said.

"And do you pack up and move to the Bahamas, leave

your business and start anew?" I asked the hard questions. Life had taught me to be a realist.

"What we have is real, Jasmine Talbot, and it doesn't come around that often. People like us are blessed to have found each other. We have to find a way."

"I agree," I told him. "I said I wanted a man just like my father. And I found him. And I said I wanted a family and children—as many as the grains of sand along the Caribbean Sea. I wanted to live in a beautiful, simple little house on the Eleuthera Islands. I didn't know that when I found that man, he'd live somewhere else."

"Your parents and grandparents made sacrifices for each other. That's what they did in order to be together."

"They certainly did."

My mother had sacrificed her entire life and career for my father. Moved to the Bahamas without a second thought. I wondered if she'd ever regretted it. Or would she have made a different choice and regretted losing him?

Jackson kissed my lips by surprise. "We have time to think about it. No hasty decisions need to be made," he said.

I stepped back and looked around. "You did an awesome job here. This place is beyond beautiful. Everyone thinks so," I told him.

"*We* did it. We were a great team." He grabbed my small hands in his. "You are the shining star here. Not me."

"Will you return for the Grand Opening?"

"I don't know that I can. I'll be working in Fort Lauderdale during that time, but I promise to try."

"Please try hard." I couldn't believe there was a question of him being here. And just after our conversation about sacrifices.

"I'll do my best," he said. "That's all I can promise, sweetheart."

I peeked through the window and saw the cabdriver parked at the curb, waiting for Jackson. Sadness overcame me, but I was brave.

"Call me as soon as you get home," I told Jackson.

"I'll call you as soon as I get in the cab." He smiled and pulled me into his arms, hugged me tightly. And then he walked away.

I watched as Jackson tossed his bags into the trunk of the car and hopped into the backseat. My heart flooded with grief. I wondered if I'd ever see Jackson again, if the calls would become less frequent and if our love affair would become like all the others I'd experienced in my life. I was used to men walking away, never to return. Tears filled my eyes as the taxi pulled away from the curb, and it felt as if my heart went with it.

Life at the Grove would be different.

I sat on the front porch with my mother and sipped tea sweetened with sugarcane. I needed to be close to my parents as I nursed my aching heart. Needed to experience their love, in order to make sense of my own.

"Things that are meant to be will be, child," said my mother. "People who love each other find ways to be together."

"When did you know that you loved Daddy?"

"The moment I met him," she said. "And that's the truth."

"Weren't you afraid to abandon your dreams to be with him? What if it didn't work out?"

"I was very afraid. I took a chance traveling from Washington, DC, to Florida. I was pregnant and scared. I wasn't sure if he'd taken up with some floozy or if he'd forgotten all about me. All I knew was that I was carrying his child and I loved him. And I knew that true love didn't come that often in a lifetime." She took a sip of her tea. "I had to take the chance."

"I've finally found my career niche with the Grove. It's where I belong. It's what I want to do for the rest of my life," I told my mother. "Are you telling me that I should abandon that for love?"

"I'm not telling you to do anything, dear." She gently rested her hand against my face. "Only you can make that decision."

"Who would run the Grove if I left?"

"You have five other siblings who have a stake in the place. One of them would have to step up."

"How would I even know that Jackson would want me there in Key West? He's a bachelor, and he's used to living alone."

"I didn't know whether or not your father would have me either. But I took a chance." My mother stood, kissed my forehead. "You don't have to decide anything tonight, Jasmine. Take your time, and think it through. Get some rest. Stop thinking so hard. You don't have to figure everything out tonight."

I would definitely think things through, but I was smart enough to know that rest wouldn't come easy.

Chapter 23

Jasmine

People traveled from all over the Bahamas and the US for the Grand Opening. Friends from college, colleagues of the Spencers, and even a few celebrities who frequented the Bahamas were in attendance. All of the Talbot children returned home for the lavish event. Alyson and Edward were the first to arrive a few days prior to the Grand Opening and helped to put the finishing touches on the event. Nate's flight arrived from Atlanta on Friday morning, followed by Whitney's that afternoon from the great state of Texas. And Denny returned home from officer's training in the United States.

Everyone dressed for the occasion in tuxedos and evening gowns. I had chosen a formfitting, sleeveless red gown—the back of it completely open and revealing my bare skin. I'd picked it up at one of the famous boutiques in Miami during a weekend visit with Alyson. We'd become much closer since our lunch in Little Havana—chatting almost every day on the phone, texting funny, quirky things to each other and getting to know each other. While in Miami, we shopped for dresses and drank mojitos at the little café that had quickly become my favorite place, too. Sisterhood was everything I'd hoped for and then some.

Everything in place, I watched as guests sipped champagne and nibbled on hors d'oeuvres. People danced casually to the sounds of Caribbean music.

I spotted my brother Edward among the crowd and walked over to him. "Hey, you."

"I'm so proud of you, Jazzy! You did an amazing job with this place," he said. "It's everything we dreamed it would be. It's perfect."

"Thank you."

"You look gorgeous, by the way." Edward hugged me tightly.

"So do you. I'm loving that tux," I said. "Thanks for believing in me."

"Honestly, I didn't think she could pull it off," Whitney said, interrupting the conversation. "I guess you proved me wrong, Jasmine Talbot."

"I guess I did." I hugged my baby sister and gave her a peck on the cheek.

"I knew she could do it all along." My father walked up, moved in between us and placed an arm around each one of us. He looked stylish in his black tuxedo.

"Oh my God, you look so handsome, Daddy!" I exclaimed and told the photographer, "Get a picture."

"Wait a minute!" Alyson rushed over. "Let me in the picture."

The photographer snapped a photo of the four of us and then Daddy gave me a strong squeeze. "You are so beautiful and so brilliant. I never doubted you for one minute."

"I know." I smiled at my father, who had been my biggest supporter.

"I surely doubted her," said Alyson. "But I have to admit, she did a fabulous job with the Grove. I'm sorry I didn't trust you at first."

"Water under the bridge," I told her. "Let's just make the best of things going forward."

"I agree," said my brother Nate, who came to see why so many Talbots were gathered in one corner of the room. "Did someone forget to invite me to the family meeting?"

"Are you still a Talbot?" I asked Nate. "Because we rarely see you on the island."

"Old wounds, my dear little sister," he said. "Sometimes they're better left unopened."

"I think I see your old wound over there across the room," said Alyson.

Nate's eyes followed her gaze. "Who invited her?" he asked.

"I invited everyone on the island," I replied.

We all glanced over at Nate's ex-girlfriend Vanessa, who was enjoying a glass of champagne and conversation with a group of people.

"You shouldn't have invited her, Jazzy. Not without asking me. You, of all people, know the history there," said Nate.

"I'm sorry."

My mother walked up wearing a formfitting silver lace gown. "I think you all need to break up this little gathering and disperse. People are starting to whisper," she said quietly.

I prayed that Nate wouldn't remain upset about my inviting Vanessa to the Grand Opening. It wasn't a deliberate attack on him, but a means for gaining more business. The Grove was marketed to everyone regardless of who they were. Word of mouth was an effective marketing tool, and Vanessa had friends.

Denny walked through the door wearing black pants and a red-wine-colored tuxedo vest. Even with his black Chuck Taylor sneakers, he still looked handsome. There was no doubt he had his own style and consistently pushed the envelope. My mother frowned when she saw his shoes. With a grin on his face, and his girlfriend, Sage, on his arm, he made his grand entrance into the party. Sage looked pretty in her red-wine-colored, knee-length dress that matched Denny's vest. The two made a handsome couple. Since he'd asked me to bring the ring, I wondered if this would be the night that he proposed to her.

Suddenly the Caribbean band that I'd hired stopped playing music, and Nate took a seat at our grandfather's grand piano. I was sure he wasn't on the program to play and wondered what he called himself doing. If this was an attempt to get the attention of his ex-girlfriend, it was neither the time nor the place. And I wouldn't stand for it. I'd worked too hard to put together a tasteful event, and I wouldn't have it ruined because of his *old wounds*.

"What are you doing?" I mouthed to him.

One of the band members offered him the microphone.

"Jazzy, can you join me over here, please?" Nate asked.

I looked over at my other siblings, who were encouraging me to go. My father gave me a nod. So I made my way to the piano and stood next to Nate.

"What are you doing?" I whispered between clinched teeth.

"I just wanted to say thank-you to my sister Jasmine for putting this wonderful event together. She's done such an awesome job here at the Grove. She prepared a great business plan for us and put together a wonderful marketing plan. She oversaw the renovation and hired and trained our staff. She is definitely the woman of the hour and deserves a round of applause."

People applauded me, and those who were seated, stood. It was overwhelming to receive such a response. I had never done anything in my life that deserved such recognition and it felt good. I'd accomplished something that I could be proud of. I glanced at my father, who stood across the room, a look of pride all over his face. It almost brought me to tears. But I was determined not to cry and ruin my makeup. It was a rare occasion that I wore any, and it wouldn't be smeared tonight. Not like the night that Alyson and I had one too many mojitos.

Nate, who was also a very talented pianist, began to play a familiar tune. It was John Legend's "All of Me," the song that Jackson had sung on our front porch so many Sundays prior.

I heard Jackson's sweet-sounding voice long before I saw him. A microphone in his hand, he stepped into the Grand Room wearing a sophisticated, steel-gray tuxedo. He stood across the room for a few moments, indulging in the sight of me as he sang the words to our beautiful love song.

Tears burned the side of my face, and I knew my makeup didn't stand a chance.

After he'd sung the last note, everyone applauded. Jackson made his way over to me and whispered in my ear, "You look gorgeous."

I was choked up, but managed to say, "I can't believe you're here." I wrapped my arms tightly around his neck.

He spoke into the microphone. "I'm so proud of you, Jasmine. The Grove is absolutely beautiful. And the work that you put in…it really proves to everyone that you're quite capable. Not that you needed to prove anything to anyone except yourself."

"You did this," I said. "You made all of this possible."

With the microphone still up to his mouth, he said, "We did it together. While working at the Grove, I learned so much about myself…about my life. But mostly about you. When I got back to Key West, I realized that there was no way I could live without you. I need you. So I sold my bungalow and put a contract on a little oceanfront property here on Eleuthera. It's a simple little place. And last night, while you were running around putting this event together, I paid a visit to your father. Your brothers were there, too. I asked your father how he would feel about me marrying his little girl…"

I looked over at my father, who gave me a wink.

"He didn't hesitate to give me his blessings. Now, your brothers, on the other hand, were a little harder to convince to give me a chance. Especially Nate, here." Jackson gave Nate a pat on the shoulder, and everyone laughed. "He was a little harder to convince than Edward and Denny. He gave me the third degree…wanted to know why I wanted to marry you so suddenly, when we haven't known each other that long."

I laughed through my tears and knew that Jackson was telling the truth. Nate was definitely overprotective.

"I explained to him that sometimes you just know when something is right, and it doesn't take very long to figure it out. I told Nate that you changed my life in such a short time and that I couldn't bear spending another day without you. Eventually, I passed his test, and here we are." He knelt on one knee.

I covered my mouth and the tears flowed harder.

"Jasmine Talbot, all of me loves all of you. Will you be my wife?"

"Yes!" I exclaimed.

Jackson stood and kissed me passionately. My mother

and sisters rushed to my side, whisked me away from Jackson and showered me with hugs.

"Oh, Jazzy, how sweet was that?" asked Whitney. "I had no idea that you were over here falling in love. Where can I get one of those?"

"I'm happy for you, sweetheart," my mother said as she handed me a glass of champagne.

"I guess we'll be planning a wedding," said Alyson. "Oh, the details! What colors will you choose? Where will you have it?"

"In the Bahamas, of course!" exclaimed Whitney. "At the Grove."

"How fitting," Alyson agreed. "You need a Vera Wang gown. I have some connections."

"Maybe in the spring, or even the summer," said Whitney.

"The fall!" exclaimed Alyson. "But sometime after hurricane season."

Jackson interrupted my sisters, who just about had my wedding planned in record time. He grabbed my hand. "Can I steal my fiancée for a moment, ladies?"

They looked at him as though he was intruding, but he managed to pull me away nonetheless. I followed Jackson to the back patio of the Clydesdale, which had been transformed into a tropical courtyard with an outside bar.

"I needed a moment alone with you. What do you think of all of this?"

"You sold your home?" I asked. "You love your home."

"I love you more."

"I had already decided I was moving to Key West. Whitney will be here in the summer to take over operations at the Grove, and I would be free to go."

"The Grove is too important for you to give up. I would never ask you to leave. Besides, Eleuthera is a much better place to raise a family."

"What about your construction business?"

"I'll run it from here. I have a great construction manager. Lance can handle the small day-to-day things. However, I might have to go away for weeks at a time when I have a job that requires me to be on-site. Can you handle that?"

"As long as I know that you're coming home to me, I can handle most anything."

"I promise not to work as hard. I won't be a workaholic," he said. "I promise you will be my priority."

"And you, mine," I swore. "My sisters already have our wedding just about planned. Do you want a big wedding or a small one? And do you want a spring or summer wedding?"

"Whatever you want, sweetheart. You just tell me where to show up, and I'll be there."

He leaned in for a kiss that rocked me to my core.

When we finally stepped back inside the Clydesdale, everyone was busy socializing and dancing to Caribbean music. My parents danced together and I watched them with admiration. I hoped Jackson and I would have a lasting love like theirs. My father gave my mother a kiss on the lips, and she smiled at him as if he was the only man in the room. I turned to my husband-to-be, gave him a kiss on the lips.

"I love you, Jackson Conner." I said it with conviction.

No doubt, Jackson was the man of my dreams, and I wanted babies with him. As many as the grains of sand along the Caribbean Sea.

* * * * *

The night
that changed
everything…

Lisa Marie Perry

When Bindi Paxton's attraction to Las Vegas Slayers legend
Santino Franco culminates in a night of passion, she knows he
could hurt her more deeply than anyone has before. But he needs
the sexy reporter to help him find his father. And as they work
together, he realizes he'd give anything for a lifetime in her arms…

THE BLUE DYNASTY

"Each character is perfectly developed and intriguing. In addition to
hot sex scenes, each character grows from the beginning of the
book to the end." —*RT Book Reviews* on *MIDNIGHT PLAY*

Available April 2015!

HARLEQUIN®
www.Harlequin.com

REQUEST YOUR FREE BOOKS!

2 FREE NOVELS PLUS 2 FREE GIFTS!

KIMANI ™
ROMANCE

Love's ultimate destination!

KPBJI700215R